Shani's eyes glazed over.

"Why is nothing in economics in plain English?"

"Let's take a step back." Logan reached across her for the textbook.

Shani scanned the text he pointed to. She scribbled down notes as fast as she could, patting herself on the back that they'd spent the better part of an hour together without her mind straying into illicit territory. Then she made the mistake of looking up at him to ask a question.

The intensity in his blue gaze stole her breath. Every resolution she'd sworn to herself evaporated in the wake of that sizzling visual connection.

She put a hand up to stop him as he leaned closer. But it somehow landed on his chest, and her fingers curled into the soft knit of his polo shirt.

His warm palm curved against her cheek, tipping back her head. And his mouth lowered to hers.

After four days of resistance, she couldn't seem to muster the strength to even whisper a *no*.

Dear Reader,

What if you had a chance to take part in a miracle? What if it was the best miracle of all—creating new life?

When a dear friend or a spouse dies unexpectedly, so much can be left unresolved. What if you had a second chance to make things right with your friend or your spouse by the simple act of bringing her child into the world?

For Shani and Logan, it means putting aside animosities between them that have existed for years. The path won't be easy for either of them, but the reward—the miracle of new life—will make up for any difficulties.

I confess, I'm a science geek, and I loved researching the world of in vitro fertilization and embryo transplants. My visit to a local fertility clinic and the embryonic lab there was a particular highlight. I hope you enjoy reading Shani and Logan's story as much as I enjoyed writing it.

Regards,

Karen Sandler

HIS MIRACLE
BATY

KAREN SANDLER

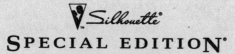

SPECIAL EDITION®

Published by Silhouette Books

America's Publisher of Contemporary Romance

SILHOUETTE BOOKS

ISBN-13: 978-0-373-24890-2
ISBN-10:   0-373-24890-3

HIS MIRACLE BABY

Books by Karen Sandler

Silhouette Special Edition

The Boss's Baby Bargain #1488
Counting on a Cowboy #1572
A Father's Sacrifice #1636
His Baby To Love #1686
The Three-Way Miracle #1733
Her Baby's Hero #1751
His Miracle Baby #1890

KAREN SANDLER

first caught the writing bug at age nine when, as a horse-crazy fourth grader, she wrote a poem about a pony named Tony. Many years of hard work later, she sold her first book (and she got that pony—although his name is Ben). She enjoys writing novels, short stories and screenplays and has produced two short films. She and her husband live in Northern California. You can reach Karen at Karen@KarenSandler.net.

To reproductive endocrinologist Dr. Laurie Lovely of the Northern California Fertility Center. Your assistance with the details of Shani and Logan's story made all the difference. Thanks so much!

Chapter One

Feeling ready to burst out of his skin, Logan Rafferty shoved the board report across his wide cherrywood desk and took an agitated look around his office. As CEO of Good Sport, the premier Sacramento area sporting-goods manufacturer, Logan merited an expansive corner space. But for the moment, despite the generous dimensions of the room, the walls seemed to be closing in on him.

When the intercom finally buzzed, it took two tries for his finger to find the speaker button. "Yes?"

"No need to bark at me, Mr. Rafferty," his matronly assistant, Mrs. Lockhart, chided him. "Ms. Jacoby is on her way up."

His edginess increased tenfold, driving him to his feet. He expected this morning's meeting would be perfunctory—he would quickly discharge his last responsibility to his late wife and then Shani Jacoby would be on her way. But Logan knew better than to count on a sure thing. Just facing Arianna's childhood friend, confronting the animosity between him and Shani that had only escalated with his wife's death a year ago, wouldn't make for a pleasant encounter.

The knock on his office door jolted him. "Come in," he said brusquely.

Mrs. Lockhart pushed the door open halfway, giving him a "behave yourself" look before she stepped inside. Shani was still hidden by the door and Logan moved to one side to watch her as she entered.

Good Lord, was she always such a knockout? Despite his better judgment, Logan stared at her, at her lush mouth, her high cheekbones, her exotic, light brown eyes. She was so slim he could span the waist of her cream-colored slacks with his hands and his palms itched to do just that. Her arms, bared by her sleeveless V-neck, were faintly sun-kissed, their warmth another temptation to touch.

Those light brown eyes narrowed on him, the lush lips pressed together. No doubt she didn't appreciate him leering at her. He gave himself a mental kick, reminding himself why Shani was here. "Thank you, Mrs. Lockhart."

His assistant gave him one last glower before she exited. Logan motioned to the chair opposite his desk. "Please, sit."

Shani did, although she perched on the edge of the soft leather chair as Logan moved around to his side of the desk. She looked past him through the floor-to-ceiling windows, at the oak-studded rolling hills visible from the fifth floor of Good Sport headquarters. When her gaze rose higher, he turned to look over his shoulder and spotted a red-tailed hawk gliding through the pale blue summer sky a moment before it dived for something in the heat-seared golden grass.

Needing something to do with his hands, he picked up a sterling-silver letter opener from his desk. It had been a gift from Arianna to celebrate Good Sport's tenth anniversary. Her way of showing him how proud she was the first year Good Sport topped twenty million in sales.

Guilt over all the ways he'd failed his late wife seemed to add weight to the ornate silver knife. In the early years of their marriage, with Good Sport struggling, threatening more than once to go under, she'd supported him without complaint. What had he given her in return?

Shani spoke finally, bringing his attention back to her. "We both know why I'm here." Her throaty voice sent sensations up his spine. "Why don't we just cut to the chase?"

She was right, of course; they might as well get this over with. He'd ask her, just as he'd promised Arianna. She'd say no and he could proceed with the plans he'd made.

He dropped the silver knife on his desk. "You're probably aware that shortly before Arianna died—" something flickered in Shani's eyes...accusation? "—we'd started four more embryos."

She dipped her head in acknowledgment. "She told me you were going to try a third time."

"I arranged to have them placed in cryopreserve. I needed the time to consider whether to proceed further with them. I've now decided to hire a gestational carrier to attempt to bring them to term." As he spoke, Shani's gaze fixed on him, as pointed as the glittering letter opener on his desk. "Before I do that, I'm duty bound to ask you first if you're willing—"

"To act as surrogate. To carry her babies." She sighed, a tantalizing sound. "Arianna and I discussed it."

"But even if you did promise her you would—"

"I didn't. I only told her I would consider it if she…" Her mouth compressed again and her gaze dropped. "If I'd known then how little time…"

"It was an accident, Shani. Nothing either of us could have predicted."

Except he and Arianna had argued that day, just before she'd driven up to Lake Tahoe. He'd run their angry words through his mind a thousand times since then, had wondered if she'd missed that curve on Highway 50 because of how upset she'd been.

Shani hooked a strand of dark brown hair behind her ear. "She wanted me to promise her, but I told her I couldn't."

Relief eased his tension. "Then I'll go ahead as planned."

He'd set things in motion three weeks ago, calling his attorney, John Evans, who'd put him in contact with a service that kept a database of potential gestational carriers. That was after John had done all he could to talk Logan out of using the embryos at all. John had been dead right—Logan was single, knew nothing about raising children and didn't have room in his life for them.

But his attorney's arguments didn't change one important fact—the burning sense of obligation within Logan to do what he could to bring these babies to term. Because he owed that much to Arianna. And he was convinced he could give his children what his own father had failed to give him—stability, respect, a sense of worth. That, more than anything, made it imperative to give them a chance at life, to show himself, show his father what parenting should be.

"Have you already found someone?" Shani asked, pulling his attention back to her. She'd locked her hands together in her lap, her arms pushing her small breasts together. The shadow between them riveted his gaze.

"Someone?" His thoughts derailed, for an instant he couldn't remember what they'd been talking about.

"A surrogate."

He forced himself to refocus on her face. Not much safer territory with that generous mouth, those intriguing light brown eyes. "I'm considering two candidates."

"Strangers."

There was no reason to feel defensive; he'd had both women thoroughly vetted. "They have excellent references."

"But how would Arianna feel, having a woman she'd never met carry her babies?"

Her tone was neutral enough, but there was a message in those soft brown eyes. That somehow, no matter how he chose, he'd be failing Arianna. Again.

"What other choice do I have?" he asked her, tamping down the sense of guilt. "You've already said you wouldn't." He didn't know why he goaded her, since her refusal was exactly what he'd wanted.

"But I haven't. I only said that Arianna left the choice up to me."

Alarm bubbled up inside him and, on its heels, irritation. "Stop playing games, Shani. I don't have the time. You have no intention of doing this." Of course she didn't. She couldn't possibly.

"Why not? I'm young and healthy."

"I don't see how a pregnancy would fit into your lifestyle. You're about to start your senior year at Sacramento State." The moment he said it, he knew it was a mistake.

She stared at him for several long moments before she spoke. "Have you been keeping tabs on me, Logan?"

He'd been curious, that was all. Once he knew he had

to contact her, he'd checked around a bit, to see what she was up to. He'd spoken to a couple of her professors and had been impressed by how hard she'd worked over the years toward her bachelor's degree—sometimes no more than a class or two a semester while working two jobs. This year had been the first she'd finally been able to take a full course load, while still working.

His interest didn't mean anything. He simply had wanted to know how stable her life was in the remote chance she'd say yes.

It was time to play his trump card, to finish this awkward encounter. "The bottom line, Shani, is that you can't. The fertility clinic won't transfer the embryos into a surrogate without a track record of pregnancy. Since you've never had a baby—"

"You're wrong."

"You can contact them yourself. Arianna may not have known that when she asked you."

"She knew. She also knew…" She shifted in her chair, her gaze drifting outside again. "I had a baby, Logan. Eight years ago, when I was eighteen."

Damn. When did Logan get so drop-dead gorgeous? That tidy dark brown hair begged for fingers to rumple it and those blue eyes cut right to her soul. Her heart pounded as she imagined what his body might feel like if she ran her hand under that well-tailored suit.

Over the years, Shani's dislike of Logan had overwhelmed any acknowledgment of his physical characteristics. When she'd last seen him a year ago at Arianna's funeral, Shani had been so swamped by grief, overwhelmed by anger, she'd had to block out Logan's presence to avoid making a scene. She'd wanted to scream at him, hit him. She'd managed to make it through that awful day knowing she would never have to face the man again.

But now, with her sorrow eased by time, it was as if a door had opened to an entirely new view of Logan. While before she had dispassionately understood her friend's attraction to her husband, now Shani experienced that magnetism firsthand. It was nothing she couldn't ignore, but it unsettled her nonetheless.

Shani had assumed Logan would never give a second thought to those embryos, which were the last memorial of her beloved friend. And if, against all odds, he did decide to bring his and Arianna's children into the world, she'd planned to simply say no to her own participation.

Except now she was here and there was nothing simple about the decision. And the prospect of giving up a final opportunity to be close to Arianna, to hold a part of her close to her heart for nine months as she'd held her own son, was unbearable. Even if it meant making a deal with the devil.

Shani forced herself to look back at Logan. He wasn't shocked at her admission—in this day and age, an unwed pregnant teenager wasn't exactly a scandal. But she saw his surprise, and suspected his view of her had altered. She'd always confronted his innate power with strength of her own. Now he'd seen a chink in her armor.

And he zeroed in on that weakness. "Where's the child now?"

She ignored the ache in her chest. "Adopted by a family back in Iowa." Of course, she didn't know if her son, eight years old now, was still in Iowa. Although it had started out as an open adoption, after three years of receiving photos of her son that had broken her heart, she'd needed a clean break.

Arianna had known exactly what she was asking when

they'd talked about the surrogacy. Could she nurture another baby inside her, knowing she would give it up? Shani had told Arianna that wouldn't be a problem.

The real issue was dealing with Logan. Overbearing, cold-blooded Logan, who'd always rubbed her the wrong way, who'd made it obvious he didn't care much for her, either. She'd had her world torn apart by a harsh, emotionless man once in her life. She wasn't about to let that happen with Logan.

He shoved his chair back and rose, no doubt hoping to intimidate her with his six-feet-plus height. "Being a surrogate isn't a cakewalk."

"Arianna told me what to expect." And she'd read up on it at the time.

He paced past her across the hardwood floor of his lavish office. "There are daily medications, oral during the prep period, by injection during the pregnancy itself."

"I'm not afraid of needles."

"You might react badly to the medication or the pregnancy itself." As he retraced his path across the office, energy seemed to sizzle off of him. "It might impact your education."

"I'll deal with it."

He stopped and towered over her. She fought the urge to stand, to try to match his height. "Once you're confirmed pregnant, you'll have to stay at my guest-house for the duration."

"No." Stay with him? That was a crazy, dangerous idea.

"It's a deal-breaker. I need to make sure the pregnancy is going well."

"Were you going to require the same of the surrogate you hired?"

"I would if they weren't both married. But it's not

necessary since they live with someone who can keep an eye on them."

Anger flared up inside her. "I don't need someone watching over me."

"Then look at it this way, Shani. If you're in the guest cottage, I can be involved in the pregnancy in a way I couldn't with the other women. These are my babies you'll be carrying."

It hit her then, with the force of a punch in the gut. She wouldn't just be nurturing Arianna's progeny for those nine months. She'd have a part of Logan inside her, as well.

Bad enough to be dealing with the man outside herself. To be pregnant with his child, to feel it growing daily, participating with him in one of the most intimate of acts between a man and woman—she must be insane to even consider it.

"Is there someone in your life you haven't told me about? Someone who would have a problem with you living on my estate?"

Shani wished she could tell him there was someone, someone tall, dark and handsome in her life to take care of her. But the only "man" sharing her bed was her cat, Seymour, and he spent most of his time curled at the foot of it, purring.

"There isn't. But what if there's a problem?" she asked. "What if a month after the doctor says I'm pregnant, what if I…" She couldn't quite say the word "miscarry" out loud.

"I'll continue to pay rent on your apartment to keep your lease current," Logan said. "You'll be able to go back at any time once you've fulfilled the surrogacy agreement."

Either by giving birth to his baby or…if she failed, that last memory of Arianna would be gone. "You don't want me doing this. Why make it easier by paying for my apartment?"

"Because Arianna would have wanted it." He looked away, then back at her, his blue eyes fierce. "Are you still willing to do this?"

She nearly told him she'd changed her mind. Why would she throw herself into a situation that would only add to the turmoil in her life?

Because of Arianna. They'd talked about it more than once, but that last time, not long before Arianna's death, the ever-present sadness in her friend's face had seemed so much more profound. The years of marriage to Logan had taken their toll.

Logan still towered over her, his broad shoulders filling her field of view. Edging her chair backward a few inches, she got to her feet, her low heels not adding much to her five-foot-eight. But unlike her dear, lost friend, she wasn't about to let herself be intimidated by this man, no matter how many inches he had on her.

"I won't let you rule my life, Logan, won't let you use my friendship with Arianna or her babies to control my actions."

He stood so close, she could barely breathe. "I couldn't care less about controlling you. I only want what's best for my embryos. To me, that means you stay at my estate."

She lifted her chin to better meet his gaze and wondered if the embryos were truly his only concern. He'd always loomed so large in Arianna's life, her friend sometimes complained she felt invisible around him.

But she wasn't Arianna. She could hold her own with Logan, no matter where she lived. "Fine. I'll live at your estate."

Was that relief in his face? Or annoyance?

"Your insurance won't pay for the medical costs."

She was glad she'd read up on the ins and outs of gestational carriers. "But you'll pay for the additional coverage, just as you would have if you'd hired a surrogate."

"Yes. I will."

Despite her misgivings, elation filled her at the prospect. "I can start any necessary treatments immediately."

She stood so close to him, she could see Logan's chest rise and fall as he breathed. She wanted to put her hands against him, to push him back, give her more space. But touching him seemed like a perilous thing to do.

He tilted his head, as if to get a better view of her face, his jaw tight. Then his gaze dropped to her mouth, lingering there. At the heat in those blue eyes, her mouth went dry and her breath caught. Bizarre fantasies crowded her mind, fragmented images of hot bare skin and sensuous moans. As the fevered thoughts bombarded her, he leaned closer. She could almost feel his mouth on hers, could feel the warmth of his breath curl against her face.

"Damn it." He wheeled away from her and strode over to the tall windows. His back to her, he stood still, his shoulders rigid.

Sinking into her chair again, Shani pressed her hands against her cheeks, horrified by what he might have seen in her face. Good God, what was she doing, lusting after Arianna's husband? Had she lost her mind? Even more preposterous, she'd almost convinced herself he was attracted to her, as well.

When he spoke, his voice was tight, controlled. "I'll make an appointment for you for Monday. You'll need a thorough physical exam as well as a psychological evaluation."

She knew that much from her research. At the moment she felt so loony she wasn't sure she could have passed any psychiatrist's tests. "Just call and let me know what time. Earlier in the day would be better than later. My morning job is more flexible."

He nodded. "I'll be speaking with you, then."

She pushed to her feet and gathered up her purse. "Leave a message if I'm not home." Another nod, apparently all the acknowledgment she was going to get. Just as well he didn't walk her to the door after they'd almost…

Almost what? Shani asked herself as she stepped out into the intense early-August heat and headed toward her teal blue Mustang. She'd simply let her imagination run away with her. For a crazed moment she'd thought he'd been about to kiss her.

Merging onto Highway 50, the morning sun glaring in her rearview mirror, Shani shook off the wild notion. This was Logan, the man she'd barely tolerated all those years he and Arianna had been married. Yes, he was good-looking, tall and well built, but her college boyfriend, Devon Masters, had been as well. What had lain behind Devon's attractive wrappings had been far uglier.

Even if she wasn't entering into this surrogacy arrangement with Logan, she truly had no inclination to get involved with a man again. Her experience with Devon when she was eighteen had made a shambles of her life and made her leery of trusting again. It had been easier over the past eight years to focus on work and school, inching toward her B.A. in business.

No wonder she'd reacted so strongly to Logan today—a woman could sublimate only so much before her libido reared its ugly head. Julie, her friend from school, probably had it right—Shani's nunlike life wasn't natural.

Just the other day, Julie had invited Shani to join a group of women from Sac State for one of their weekly Friday-evening get-togethers. Shani wasn't much for the bar scene, but maybe she ought to give Julie a call. A night out with the girls might be just the thing to take her mind off Logan.

Because after Monday, assuming all went well with her medical exams and evaluations, everything in Shani's life would change. If she was going to build her armor against Logan, she'd better do it now, before her world turned upside down.

Chapter Two

The two-plus months it took for Shani's body to be ready for the embryo transfer dragged by for Logan, torturously slow. The anticipation distracted him at work, disrupted his sleep, set a razor edge to his temper. There were nights it was all he could do to keep from rising from bed and howling at the moon in frustration.

Now, with Shani beside him in his Mercedes, terror replaced frustration, misgivings and second thoughts piling up in his mind. The beautiful late-September morning, with its golden sunshine and brilliant blue sky, was lost on him. Thunderstorms and gloom would have better matched his mood.

Arianna would have seen the gorgeous weather as a kind of sign that it was a good day to start a baby. He glanced over at Shani, sitting silently beside him, and wondered whether she saw portents in the day.

Over the past two months, his contacts with her had

been limited to phone calls and e-mails. There'd been no need to see her; she drove herself to the fertility clinic as needed and the nurse he'd hired took care of the twice-weekly estrogen shots. He'd been busy in any case with business travel and endless meetings. He'd wanted to clear the decks for a lighter workload during Shani's pregnancy, make it possible to have a few of his VPs stand in for him as needed.

Although their visits were short and they spoke little, thoughts of her occupied far too many of his waking moments. If the pregnancy took and he moved her to the guest cottage, it would only get worse. It shouldn't matter; they would have nothing more than a business relationship. But the thought of having her so close just added to his edginess.

A delicate floral scent drifted toward him, tantalizing him. "Are you wearing perfume?"

She glanced toward him, her eyes wide. "Of course not. The doctor said I shouldn't."

Just his imagination, then. If he couldn't control it during these few minutes in the car with her, how would he keep himself in line for nine months?

He diverted his focus to the upcoming embryo-transfer procedure, but that only shredded his nerves more. For months now, he'd mulled over the success-rate statistics for frozen embryo transfers. And he had experienced the failures firsthand with Arianna. Although her pregnancy took the second time, his late wife had lost the baby in the first six weeks. His difficulties in getting along with Shani could be a moot point if the procedure wasn't successful.

That thought struck him like a knife edge to the gut. It didn't bear thinking about. This might not be his last chance for children, but it certainly would be his last opportunity to expiate his various sins committed against his late wife. He had to hope at least one of the four embryos would grow and thrive inside Shani.

At the clinic, he parked near the door and shut off the engine, amazed to find his hand shaking as he pulled the key from the ignition. Shani's fingers rested lightly on his wrist. "It'll be okay," she said.

He could feel that slight touch curling up his arm, nesting in his chest. An ache settled in the vicinity of his heart, urging him to tug her into his arms, to hold her, feel her arms around him.

He broke the contact abruptly, exiting the car. Leaning against the Mercedes, he struggled to pull himself together, baffled by his moment of weakness. No doubt a consequence of too much stress and too little sleep.

Shani had climbed out and she watched him across the roof. He expected curiosity in her light brown gaze; her empathy nearly did him in. He turned away and started for the clinic door, waiting for her to catch up.

Another couple sat in the waiting room, clutching each other's hands, gazing into each other's eyes. The man brushed a kiss on the woman's temple, then murmured something in her ear. The woman smiled and leaned closer to him.

The first time Logan had come here with Arianna, he'd taken her hand, but she'd pulled away. She'd told Logan that his touching her just made her more nervous. She'd moved two seats away and flipped through a magazine as they'd waited. He'd ended up spending most of the time on the phone, thrashing out one problem or another to keep his mind off the upcoming procedure.

He wondered if Shani would feel the same way Arianna had. She'd said so little this morning, he had no idea how she felt. He should ask her, make sure she was still committed to the procedure. But she would have told him if she wasn't, wouldn't she?

He never got the chance to ask. After they'd signed in, Dr. Conners, the reproductive endocrinologist, arrived almost immediately to take them into her office. The two women led the way, Shani behind the salt-and-pepper-haired forty something doctor. As Logan followed Shani, he kept his eyes fixed on the back of her head, not allowing his gaze to drift down to watch the beguiling sway of her hips.

Dr. Conners gave Shani a consent form to read and sign, then handed Logan three photographs. "We were able to successfully thaw three of the four embryos in cryopreserve."

Logan stared down at the black-and-white photos of blastocysts, the five-day-old embryos he and Arianna had created and frozen a year ago. He'd been through this part of the procedure twice before with Arianna. Her joy, her burgeoning hope had been obvious. She'd expected that same anticipation and excitement from him, but he never seemed to be able to muster up those emotions.

Why would it be any different this time? The ability to feel that instant connection Arianna had experienced just wasn't in him. The collection of cells intrigued him, but he'd felt the same dispassionate interest studying the chemical formula for the new polymer in Good Sport's latest-model racquetball.

He passed the photos over to Shani. Smiling, she scrutinized the curves and mounds on the printed images. "What a miracle that we all start like this."

He considered telling her it was just biology… science. But even he didn't entirely believe that. These tiny scraps of genetics, nurtured inside Shani's body, could become his sons or daughters. Considering the father who raised him, he might have had the lousiest role model for being a parent, but that potential life meant something, even to him.

Dr. Conners set two bottles of water on the desk. "Drink them down, Ms. Jacoby. They'll give us a good window for the ultrasound."

Shani finished the first one, then wiped her mouth. He almost touched her then, to swipe the last drop of moisture from her lower lip. Instead, he clenched his hands in his lap.

Shani smiled as she set aside the bottle. "I hope I don't have to wait too long for the bathroom afterward."

"Not too long," Dr. Conners said. "Go ahead and change. Mr. Rafferty will meet you in the preop room."

Logan rose to follow Shani, but the doctor put a hand on his arm to stop him. "I just want to make sure you understand the odds of success, Mr. Rafferty. Although Ms. Jacoby is a good candidate, young and healthy, your wife was nearly thirty-five when the embryos were created. The odds aren't as good for an older donor nor for frozen embryo transfer."

"I've been through this before. And I've read the statistics. It's not as if I have an alternative."

"Then we'll hope for the best." The doctor walked him out. At the door to the procedure area, she handed him paper booties and a hat to put on before they entered.

He rapped on the door to the preop room, waiting for Shani's "Come in" before he entered. She lay on the bed in a hospital gown, a sheet pulled over her, her arms on top alongside her body. The bones of her wrists were so delicate, the lines of her face so dainty, she seemed incredibly fragile.

A strand of hair clung to her cheek and without

thinking, he stroked it back behind her ear. Her eyes widened and he broke the contact. "Sorry," he muttered.

"Are you nervous?" she asked.

He was, even more than he'd been the previous two times. "You're the one going through a medical procedure."

She laced her fingers on her flat belly. "The procedure doesn't worry me. It's the results…but I shouldn't think too far ahead, I guess." Her legs shifted under the sheet. "Was Arianna nervous?"

"Yes." He didn't want to remember Arianna lying in that bed, a mass of excited nerves—and his impotence in calming her. She'd let him hold her hand at that point, but he knew it wasn't enough. Nothing he did ever seemed to be.

The nurse came then to take them to the embryo-transfer room. Hooking a mask on over his ears, Logan walked alongside the bed, Shani's gaze steady on his. He wished he could absorb a tenth of the serenity he could see in her face.

Once they had her bed in position in the transfer room, she stretched out her hand toward him. "Do you mind? I guess I'm more nervous than I thought."

Inexplicably, her palm against his calmed him. He wondered if that had been Shani's intention.

Dr. Conners moved the ultrasound screen into position, so they could all watch the procedure. She pressed the paddle against Shani's belly, and an incomprehensible image was displayed on the ultrasound screen.

"Here's the bladder and the uterus," the doctor said, indicating bright spots within what looked like static. "You'll see the embryo transfer catheter in just a moment."

Shani's grip tightened as the doctor picked up the catheter containing the three embryos. The seven-inch flexible tube was attached to a syringe, the embryos in the tip, ready to be transferred.

He folded Shani's hand into both of his as Dr. Conners inserted the catheter. "Watch that thin white line," she told them.

He focused on the fuzzy jumble of light and made out the line Dr. Conners had described as it grew longer on the screen. He leaned close to Shani. "You'll see a white dot. That's the embryos."

At the brief flare of light, Shani's hand squeezed even harder. "I see it." She lifted her gaze to him, smiling.

"Shani…" He fought the urge to raise her hand to his face, to press it against his cheek. "Thank you."

Logan pulled up in front of Shani's apartment complex and put a hand over hers as she unbuckled her seat belt. "Wait."

"I can walk inside on my own."

"Humor me," he told her as he climbed from the car.

With a sigh, Shani pushed aside her seat belt and watched Logan round the front of the car. She let him open the door—he'd probably think she'd strain something if she did it herself—then took his hand. He nearly lifted her out of her seat.

When he took her arm to guide her toward her apartment, she'd had enough. She snatched her arm back and shouldered past him along the walkway. "I'm not an invalid, for heaven's sake."

He glowered down at her as he dogged her steps. "Dr. Conners said three days' bed rest."

"She also said I could walk to the bathroom, take a shower." She jabbed her key into the door of her ground-floor apartment. "Were you planning to be there for that, too?"

She wanted to bite back the words as soon as she said them. The air seemed to grow heavy between them and graphic images flooded her mind—Logan undressing her, stepping into the shower with her. A flush burned her cheeks as she shoved open the door, startling her cat, Seymour, from his nap on the back of the sofa.

Logan shut the door behind him, in no apparent hurry to leave. "The nurse's aide will be continuing with your shot regimen. Progesterone every day now in addition to the twice-a-week estrogen."

"We arranged for her to be here at eight every morning before I leave for my job at the library." Shani set her purse down on the sofa and ran a hand down Seymour's back. The cat, no doubt feeling her edginess, jumped to the floor and stalked off to the bedroom.

Logan looked around Shani's small, plainly furnished living room, his gaze abruptly coming to a stop at the portrait of Arianna as a girl. The oil painting, along with a few other keepsakes Arianna had asked to be given to Shani, had arrived in the mail three months after Arianna's death. The package had included no personal note from Logan, just a tersely worded letter from the probate attorney.

Logan returned his attention to Shani. "My housekeeper, Mrs. Singh, will be bringing you your meals over the weekend."

"She really doesn't need to. I can just order takeout for delivery." Shani headed into her bedroom, hoping that would be enough of a hint for Logan to go home.

He didn't take the hint, crossing the living room to stand over her. "I don't want you eating junk food."

She stepped away from him and pulled back the covers on the bed. "Excuse me, I have to change." When he didn't move, she tugged the hem of her T-shirt from her jeans.

Logan backed out hastily. "I'll give Mrs. Singh a call to make sure she's on her way."

Shani hurried across the bedroom to swing the door shut, pressing her back against it as if she could keep at bay the sensations rioting along her nerves. She dragged in a long breath, blanking her mind. Seymour jumped on the bed and eyed her with a cat's avid fascination.

"Just me being an idiot," she told the cat, then yanked off her T-shirt and skinned out of her jeans.

Digging through her dresser, she searched for something decent to wear. She'd had a weakness for slinky nighties since she was a teenager, the skimpier, the better. No one had shared her bed for more than a year, but she still collected bright-colored scraps of silk and lace, nearly filling a dresser drawer with them.

She pulled out the most conservative confection, a scarlet teddy and matching tap pants. She doubted Logan's housekeeper would find it terribly shocking to see her wearing them.

But what if Logan stayed until Mrs. Singh arrived? She knew he'd intended to go in to work once he had her settled in. But maybe he'd have some parting scold before he left her in peace.

She'd better go for more coverage than the teddy. Digging through the drawer, she found the thigh-length T-shirt she usually wore over her swimsuit and threw it on. Once she'd crawled into bed and pulled up the sheet, everything was safely concealed.

Earlier, she'd stacked her textbooks on the nightstand with a pad and pens. If she couldn't do anything else this weekend, she might as well get ahead on her reading assignments. Pillows plumped more comfortably behind her, she scanned the course syllabus for her industrial organization class.

The text was third in the stack. When she pulled it free, the pile shifted, and the two top books clattered to the floor.

"Shani?" Logan called from the living room. "Are you all right?"

"I'm fine!" She leaned over the edge of the bed, her T-shirt sliding up past her waist. She nabbed one book but couldn't quite reach the other.

"I'm coming in," Logan called out an instant before he opened the bedroom door. He stared at her dangling over the edge of the bed. "What the hell are you doing?"

She tried to push herself back up, but the T-shirt caught on the edge of the bed, sliding up even farther. She had only to look up at Logan's face to see she'd exposed more than her rib cage.

Moving slowly, he went down on one knee to take the book from her hand, then set it with the other on the stack. His gaze locked with hers as Shani eased herself back against the pillows. Praying he'd leave, hoping he wouldn't, Shani watched, mesmerized as he straightened, then sat on the edge of the bed.

Her T-shirt was still rucked up around her waist, and she thought as he reached for her that he'd just pull it back into place. But then he laid his hand against the bare skin just above her panties, and she felt as if she would drown in Logan's heat.

Logan should have turned his back the moment Shani's T-shirt slid into dangerous territory, should have let her right herself and make herself decent again. But the view of the creamy underside of her breast, the way the hem had caught on her nipple, giving him only the barest glimpse of her rose-dimpled areola, made his libido take charge. Without conscious thought, he was on that bed beside her, his hand spread at her waist, the soft warmth of her skin like paradise against his palm.

He could still put on the brakes. Didn't have to lean closer. He had at least that much self-control. But with Shani's soft lips parted, her gaze dropping to his mouth, her breath releasing in a sigh, dredging up willpower seemed like a ridiculous notion.

He only needed one small brush of his mouth against hers, just to see if her lips were as satiny as they looked. It didn't have to go any further than that.

Her eyes fluttered closed as he lowered his head. He felt her hand on his arm, moving along the bare skin below the sleeve of his polo shirt. Her slender fingers wrapped around his biceps, burning into his skin.

He had only to ease his hand higher and he could run his thumb along the underside of her breast. Her breasts were small now, more petite than Arianna's had been, but later, if the embryo transfer was successful, they would swell, grow riper, more luscious—

His rampant thoughts jolted to a stop as cold awareness slapped him in the face. Stumbling to his feet, Logan backed away from Shani. She stared up at him, her brown eyes wide and startled, her lips parted.

That was nearly enough to pull him back to her, but she tugged down her shirt and yanked the covers nearly to her chin. He could see the pink tinting her cheeks, could imagine how warm they would feel to his touch.

Her gaze slid away from him. "I have to study."

He tried to order his thoughts, scrambling for something to focus on other than joining Shani in that bed. "I have to get to work." He had no idea how he'd be able to concentrate on anything the rest of the day except Shani and what her mouth might have felt like.

She took the top book from the stack beside her and

plopped it on her lap. Her gaze lifted to his and he saw the expectation in her eyes. He entertained a brief fantasy about what that look meant—that she wanted him close again, that she needed his touch.

But then her brow furrowed. "I need to study," she said more firmly.

He gave himself a mental kick in the rear and turned away from her. "Mrs. Singh should be here any minute."

As he walked back to the car, he wished he could rewind the last few minutes. Damn. How could he have been such an idiot, especially with so much at stake? It would serve him right if she refused to allow him unchaperoned visits with her for the next nine months.

As he slammed the Mercedes' door shut, he spied the images of the blastocysts Shani had left on her seat. Staring down at the fuzzy gray images, Logan reflected that this was all that was left of his legacy with Arianna, a final fragment of their union. A clear reminder that he had to find a way to behave like a grown-up with Shani. And respect Arianna's memory in the process.

Chapter Three

Once Shani finished the three days of bed rest, she dove back into her life, doing her best to forget what had nearly happened between her and Logan in her bedroom. Between her morning job at the university library, her afternoon classes and her Fridays and Saturdays at a local print shop, she had little time to dwell on that charged moment of intimacy. When thoughts of Logan did intrude, she redirected her mind to the three embryos growing inside her, sending them all the positive energy she could.

Six days after the embryo transfer, on Thursday, Shani reported to the fertility clinic for the first of two blood draws to be used for the initial pregnancy test. The clinic had frozen that first blood sample, then would compare it to this morning's sample, taken two days later. The doctor would be checking the pregnancy hormone level in the blood sometime between one and two this afternoon and determine if it had risen sufficiently between the two draws.

Shani had gone directly from the clinic to the print shop, figuring she could keep her mind occupied with her usual Saturday routine. But as the morning wore on, she bounced between despair and joy as she waited to hear from Logan. As the father, he'd be notified first of the results of the pregnancy test, then she assumed he'd call her. Since she hadn't seen him at all since the transfer, she wasn't sure. For all she knew, she'd find a note on her apartment door when she got home... *By the way, you're pregnant.*

By eleven, her distraction was driving her crazy. Closing her mind to everything else, she threw herself into the stock inventories and accounts receivable reports the owner had requested she take care of this morning. By the time she came up for air, it was one-thirty.

She could just imagine Logan's disapproval if he found out she'd skipped lunch. As she dithered over whether to go next door to the little market for a snack or to go out to lunch, she heard the front door beep. Rolling her chair over to peek through the office door, Shani checked to make sure Roy heard the door chime. A few minutes ago, Roy had been buried in the bowels of a copy machine, trying to convince it to keep running until the repairman could get there.

She spotted Roy, hefting a full box of copy paper heading for the counter. He greeted the customer with a polite "How can I help you, sir?"

Except it wasn't a customer. It was Logan, looking larger than life in well-fitted slacks and a dress shirt with rolled-up sleeves. Pacing the length of the counter, he looked past Roy, no doubt searching for her. Shani's heart kicked into high speed in anticipation of whatever news he was here to deliver.

Rising from her chair, she stepped up to the counter. "Thanks, Roy. This is a friend of mine." He wasn't, really. But it was simpler than explaining her true relationship with Logan.

"Did the doctor call?" Shani asked, excitement making her voice thready.

But Logan seemed fixed on Roy lugging the box of paper to the copier. "Do you carry those? They must weigh fifty pounds."

"That's Roy's job. I don't carry boxes around."

His fingers tightened on the edge of the counter. "I don't want you lifting anything that heavy."

"I don't." Shani took a breath. "What did the doctor say?"

He met her gaze finally, his hand slipping across the counter to cover hers. "The test was positive. You're pregnant."

She couldn't hold back her smile or the burst of elation inside her. "That's great. That's wonderful." She turned her hand to link her fingers with his.

"There was a good rise in the hormone level between the two samples." His grip tightened. "You won't need another test for ten days."

She remembered that was a positive sign. "I'm so happy for you, Logan."

"It's early days yet," he reminded her. "How many hours are you working?"

The sudden change of subject threw her for a loop. "Sixteen hours here, sixteen at the library."

"We need to talk."

"About the move to the guesthouse?"

"Another issue. Can you take a break?"

"I was about to leave for lunch." Before he could scold her for waiting so long to eat, she added, "I lost track of time."

Nevert[h]
thing to do
that I shou[ld]
His ga[ze]
answer. He
bread plate
"Ariann[a]
"And ne
under my r
"Doing
soap opera
"You ca[n]
Even wh
wanted to j
world, she
and someti
home when
or her siste[r]
She was
fixed her ga[ze]
Irritation
this later.''
"No." She
be sure she
"Damn it
He turne[d]
His blue ey[es]
Then both e
The first t
thought was
tender skin
Logan had
business enj
She pulled

ing as startled as she felt. Too rattled to think straight, she blurted out a question she'd been rolling around in her mind these past two-plus months. "Why are you doing this?"

Color rose in his cheeks, and she realized he'd misunderstood her question. "Doing what?"

"Why have a baby at all?"

"Why wouldn't I?"

"I got the impression from Arianna that she was the one who wanted children, not you."

"She told you that?"

"Not in so many words." Shani tried to remember what Arianna *had* said. *He's a hard man, Shani. Sometimes I wonder if I'm doing the right thing bringing children into this marriage.*

He picked up his slice of bread and tore the crust from it. "I think we wanted children for different reasons."

"Then why?" she pressed.

"Why ask this now?" he countered. "You're committed. You can't change anything. If my reasons don't meet your approval—"

"I don't approve or disapprove."

"Then I think this subject is closed, as well." He set down his bread, uneaten. "I'd like to move you to the cottage tomorrow. Is ten o'clock too early?"

"No," she said, jolted by the door he'd slammed in her face. "Ten o'clock is fine."

Because of the animosity between her and Logan, Shani had limited her visits to Arianna's home in Sacramento's Fabulous Forties district. They would meet at the college for lunch, at Shani's apartment on evenings when Logan worked late or at a restaurant for dinner. Shani had never even seen the Granite Bay estate Logan had bought his wife a year before her death. She only knew that Arianna had never liked it, had never felt comfortable there.

As she followed Logan's Mercedes from her apartment to the estate, Shani tried to imagine what the house would look like—some kind of fussy Tudor, maybe, with brick turrets and false timbering. Or a Greek Revival, with white columns and an imposing entryway.

She passed between the two massive oaks that flanked the gated entry to the six-acre property. The house, up on a hill and behind a thick cluster of oaks, wasn't visible at first. It wasn't until Shani's car topped the last grassy rise that she got her first glimpse of Logan's home.

Not a Tudor, or Greek Revival. Instead, it could have been a farmhouse in Iowa.

Granted, this farmhouse was bigger than anything standing in a cornfield back home. If there were as many bedrooms inside as the outside suggested, the place could house a large family and all their hired hands comfortably. Even still, its wide, inviting front porch, dormer windows on the second floor and fresh, white-painted clapboards gave her an immediate sense of homecoming.

They continued past the house to the guest cottage, separated from the farmhouse by an expanse of green lawn. She smiled with delight when she saw the cottage. It was a converted barn, styled like a miniature of the house, down to the dormer windows in the roof. The three Dutch doors that had once led to the stalls had been left in place, the upper doors replaced by windows. She could almost imagine the horses poking their noses out, hoping for a carrot.

She slid from her car. "It's lovely," Shani told Logan as he walked toward her.

Her compliment surprised a smile out of Logan. "I'm glad you like it."

His patience at being confined to a cat carrier worn out, Seymour started yowling from the passenger seat. Intent on rescuing her cat, Shani shut the door and started toward the other side of the car.

As she stepped between the two vehicles, she nearly collided with Logan, busy pulling boxes out of the trunk of the Mercedes. "Sorry." She sidled around him and rescued Seymour.

Two boxes stacked in his arms, he trailed after her to the cottage. "Since Mrs. Singh isn't here, I've made dinner reservations for seven o'clock."

She stared at his back as he set down the boxes and unlocked the cottage. "You know, I did manage to feed myself before you came along."

"I can change it to seven-thirty if it's more convenient." He set the boxes down, then walked past her to get another load from the car.

Setting Seymour's carrier down beside her, Shani turned to scan the cottage interior. A living room took up half of this end of the converted barn, a kitchenette and breakfast nook filled the other half. The dormers were set in the vaulted ceiling, sunshine spilling through them, lighting the space. She smiled, completely content with her temporary home.

Seymour was not quite so complacent. He yowled again, his golden gaze pleading for freedom through the metal grate of the carrier. "Okay, fuzz face, I'll let you out," she told the cat, then carried him to the bedroom. That cozy room had been carved out of the back of the barn and had a compact bathroom adjoining it.

Fishing through one of the boxes Logan had brought in, she found the litter pan and sand and set it up in the bathroom. With the bedroom door shut, she released Seymour, and watched for a moment as he crept from the carrier. She left him to sniff the bed.

Still with her eye on Seymour to make sure he didn't escape the bedroom, she didn't realize Logan was on the other side of the door until she backed into him. Her suitcases dropped on either side of him as he reached up to steady her. She shut the door quickly to keep the cat in and found herself sandwiched between an unyielding doorjamb and a warm male body. Logan's hands wrapped around her arms, his fingertips barely an inch from her breasts.

She could have easily shrugged away from him, broken the connection. But with the feel of his chest pressed against her back and her rear cupped deliciously against him, she couldn't seem to move. She wanted to arch her neck, to lean back against his shoulder, to listen to his heart and see if his was beating as fast as hers.

Thankfully, he backed away. "I thought you'd want your suitcases in the bedroom."

She dropped her gaze to the two pieces of baggage, uneasy about what she might see in his face. "We can leave them here. I just let the cat out."

She finally lifted her gaze to his, and his intense blue eyes sent sensation tingling up her spine. "Shani…"

Just her name, in that low, deep voice. It was as much a caress as the touch of his hands. She could barely muster breath for a response. "Yes?"

Only a few feet separated them, still within reach if they both stretched out their arms. His hands opened as if he was about to do just that.

He took a step back. "We can't do this."

"No." She shook her head for emphasis. "And what happened back at the apartment…"

"That was a mistake. I never should have…"

"I agree."

"It was my fault," he said. "It won't happen again."

"We'll just forget it," Shani said, "and go from here." Except she had no idea if she could forget.

He backed toward the door. "I'll pick you up at six-thirty, then."

"No."

His eyes flared wider. "Don't be obstinate."

"You said Mrs. Singh stocked the refrigerator. I'll make myself something." She put up a hand to forestall the argument she could see him about to launch. "I'm tired, Logan. I need some time to get settled in."

In that moment, she felt exhausted, the past two months of stress coupled with surging emotions from the hormone injections piling up on her. As the pregnancy progressed—assuming nothing went amiss—she would be even more worn out. She'd better get her rest now while she could.

His jaw worked, mouth compressing. "Another time, then. I'm taking a red-eye to New York tomorrow night. It's a trip I couldn't get out of. Mrs. Singh will be here to take care of you."

She would have reminded him she didn't need taking care of, but didn't want to risk another confrontation. "I'll see you when you get back, then."

He gave her a curt nod. "Let me show you how the alarm system works. I want you to set it before you go to bed at night and every time you leave."

She moved up beside him, keeping as much space between them as she could and still see the small control box. He rattled off the activation code, had her repeat it back to him. Then after demonstrating the proper sequence to activate the alarm, he stood over her and watched her copy his actions.

Finally satisfied she understood the system, he turned and walked out, shutting the door behind him. Shani shivered at the memory of him holding her outside her bedroom, at the way he'd said her name. She'd seen a message in his eyes, an intriguing puzzle she burned to solve.

She should have been grateful he would be gone for a day or two. With everything in her life topsy-turvy, she wouldn't have the added complication of Logan's presence.

Instead she felt unaccountably lonely.

Chapter Four

Ten days later, as Shani finished her breakfast of juice and one of Mrs. Singh's cranberry muffins, she spotted Logan walking past the cottage window. Taking a last bite, she opened the door for him.

"I only have a minute," she said as she turned back to clear the table. "I have to stop at the clinic before I head to school."

Glancing back over her shoulder, she caught him staring at her. She wondered if she'd buttoned her Hawaiian shirt wrong, or if she hadn't quite tamed the morning's bed hair.

"How have you been doing?" he asked.

She'd barely seen him these past several days and only from afar. Sometimes, as she left for school, he was out on his front porch. In the evening, as she ate her dinner, she'd see his car pull into the driveway.

So his presence this morning surprised her. She set

her plate and glass in the dishwasher and swiped crumbs from the counter into the sink.

"I'm fine. I'm visiting the vampire this morning." She'd jokingly called the phlebotomist that during the first blood draw and the woman had been delighted with the nickname. "They'll call you later with the results." Shani was grateful this third test of her hormone levels was the last.

"There's something I want to talk to you about."

"Not about quitting working, I hope."

He looked away. "You made yourself clear on that point."

She reached for her backpack, but he hefted it out of her reach. "I told you before, I don't like you carrying anything this heavy."

"It weighs twenty pounds," she told him. "I tested it on the bathroom scale."

She held her hand out for her backpack, but he didn't relinquish it. Snatching up her purse, she hurried from the cottage. He followed her out to the car, opening the door for her and tossing her backpack on the passenger seat.

"I really don't have the time for lectures right now. After the clinic, I'm meeting my adviser about my senior thesis."

He stood by the car door, close enough that she'd have to brush against him to get in the car. "Are you free for dinner?"

She waited a moment, hoping he would back away. He didn't move, so she squeezed her slim body between him and the doorjamb. "I was planning to study."

He leaned down to eye level. "I'll order dinner and we can eat here. I won't take much of your time. I can let you know about the pregnancy test, as well."

The urgency to leave battled with the temptation to

lift her face to his. But why? To have him kiss her? That made no sense. It must be the early-morning hour, coupled with caffeine deprivation.

"Fine," she said. "Dinner. Six-thirty."

He stepped back and shut her door. She could still feel his gaze on her, as tangible as his touch might have been, until she drove down the steep driveway and out of sight.

When she returned home after her industrial organization class, exhausted from the day and with barely twenty minutes before Logan was due to arrive, she found a note taped to the door of the cottage. She recognized the handwriting as Mrs. Singh's. Logan's housekeeper occasionally left her notes to let her know when she'd be doing the shopping. Shani would write her grocery list on the back and leave the note taped to the door.

But Mrs. Singh had just been to the supermarket the day before. Slinging her backpack over her shoulder, she tugged the note free of the door. *Mr. Rafferty will be late,* the note read. *Please expect him at seven-thirty.*

A little annoyed that Logan had gotten the last word on when dinner would be, she was nevertheless relieved to have time for a shower and maybe even a quick nap. Slipping inside, she filled Seymour's bowl, then undressed in the bedroom. She showered in record time, then pulled on panties and a bra before climbing into bed.

As she snuggled under the covers, she fretted briefly over how her wet hair would dampen the pillowcase. But the comfortable bed coupled with the long day sent her almost immediately into a deep sleep.

She dreamed she was at the university, walking into her principles of marketing class. There was no one else in the room and she thought in sudden panic she must be late. When she looked again, she saw babies on every desk, all of them hollering. At the front of the classroom, her professor had morphed from the dour-faced Dr. Maass into Logan. He shouted her name over the sound of the babies crying and pounded on the professor's desk.

She walked toward him, grabbing his hands so he'd stop making such a racket. His eyes blazing down at her, he leaned down, his mouth covering hers, his hands cradling her face….

She jolted awake, the blankets falling from her as she sat up. Struggling to focus on the bedside clock, she saw it was a quarter to eight. Then she registered the sound of the front door opening.

Her heart, already racing, skipped even faster as she leaped from the bed. Before she shut the bedroom door, she caught a glimpse of Logan entering the cottage, white plastic bags in his hands. She'd been so sound asleep, she didn't hear his knock.

"Be out in a minute," she yelled through the door, then leaned against it to catch her breath. Images from her dream still whirled in her mind. She shook her head to clear it, then unearthed a pair of jeans and a sweater.

A glance in the mirror informed her she never should have napped with damp hair, but she managed to tidy it somewhat. Scooting her feet into slippers, she left the safety of her bedroom.

"Sorry. I fell asleep."

The sleeves of his pale blue dress shirt were rolled up, exposing the taut muscling of his arms. The feel of his hands on her face in the dream had been so real, she could almost feel the warmth lingering. A flush rose in her cheeks in reaction.

He gave her a quick once-over, setting off even more heat. "Are you feeling okay?"

"Sure. Just a little tired."

His gaze narrowed on her hair. "It's sticking up." Before she could move out of reach, he was stroking the side of her head, the real touch tangling with images from her dream. "That's better."

She told herself she was imagining the huskiness of his voice, the way he seemed to be lingering over smoothing the stray lock. The moment he dropped his hand, a puzzling mix of relief and regret competed inside her.

She redirected her attention to the white boxes on the table. "Chinese?" she asked. He'd already set out plates.

"From Madam Fong's. Sit. I'll get you milk."

As hungry as she was, she wasn't about to argue. She served up steaming plates of orange chicken and broccoli beef, then scooped some white rice beside them.

Once he'd set down her milk and a glass of ice water for himself, Logan sat opposite her. "The pregnancy test was positive. The hormone levels look good."

She picked up a piece of beef with her chopsticks. "Now we only have to wait eight more months."

"Arianna lost the baby at six weeks."

The beef tasted like ashes in her mouth at the memory. If she started thinking about what-ifs, it would make her crazy.

Better to change the subject.

"All the years I knew Arianna, she never said much about how you met," Shani said after a pause.

"It's not much of a story."

"That's what she said. I'd like to hear it anyway."

"Her mother was a friend of my mother."

"I thought your mother died when you were young."

"When I was seven." He pushed the orange chicken around on his plate but didn't take a bite.

"That must have been hard." Shani's mother was so

important in her life, she couldn't imagine growing up without her.

"I barely remember her. Arianna and I played together as children, but we lost touch. She contacted me not long after I started Good Sport."

Shani knew that Good Sport, a designer and manufacturer of upscale sporting goods equipment, had been in existence for twelve years. The company had just been taking off seven years ago when Shani met Arianna. Then three years ago Logan had locked up contracts for custom equipment for the NHL and NFL, and Good Sport had flown into the stratosphere.

Two years later, Arianna was dead. She'd gotten such a brief taste of Logan's success.

"What about your father?" Shani asked.

The barest flicker of a reaction flashed across his face, a trace of anger at the mention of his father. "Lives in the Bay Area. Your family's all still in Iowa?"

"Most of them. My mother and my sister. My grandmother. Some aunts and uncles and cousins."

"Have you told your mother yet?" he asked.

She shook her head. "I'll tell her in another month. We'll be more certain then."

He scooped up some rice. "What about your father?"

"He left my mother when I was twelve." The bitterness she felt at his betrayal had faded over the years, but she couldn't quite squelch it entirely. "We haven't heard from him since."

"Then we have that in common," Logan said. "Absent parents."

He looked around him at the cozy living area adjacent to the tiny kitchen table. "You've settled in, I see."

Over the weekend she'd gone back to the apartment to pick up a few things—colorful pillows for the small sofa, an old quilt her grandmother had made in the fifties when she'd been a new bride, a few photographs of her sister and mother. The portrait of Arianna hung in a place of pride over the sofa.

She'd never known Arianna as a child, but seeing that sweet, smiling face never failed to lift Shani's spirits. "I wanted it to feel a little more like home."

Logan's gaze fixed on the portrait. "Arianna always liked it here. When she and I…" He shrugged. "She'd come over here, spend a few hours alone."

Shani's heart ached at the thought of her friend's loneliness. "You had something you wanted to talk to me about."

Logan set down his chopsticks. "First, I want you to hear me out before you refuse."

"Is this about me working? I thought we'd settled that."

"There's an opportunity for you to come work at Good Sport as a paid intern."

She narrowed her gaze on him suspiciously. "Doing what?"

"We have an incubator of sorts set up, an offshoot of Good Sport's R and D department. Clint Ferguson, one of the business analysts in the unit, has been budgeted for an assistant but hasn't had the time to hire anyone."

In spite of herself, she was intrigued. "How many hours a week?"

"Twenty instead of the thirty-two you're working now. But the pay will be greater to make up for the decreased hours." He fidgeted with the chopsticks. "In addition, Clint's been planning a set of substantial studies that would probably dovetail nicely into a senior thesis."

Talk about an offer she couldn't possibly refuse. Although she enjoyed the library work and her time at the print shop, neither would look as good on her résumé as a stint as an intern at Good Sport. "This isn't your way of easing me out of working entirely, is it? You won't snatch this out from under me after I've quit my other jobs?"

He seemed offended. "I wouldn't do that."

Could she trust him? Arianna had complained so many times of broken promises. Would he keep his word?

Of even more concern, Shani didn't like being so beholden to him, didn't like him intruding on yet another aspect of her life. She was living under his roof, she was carrying his babies, now she'd be employed by his company. How tightly could she let him be woven into her life before she lost the sense of who she was?

As she hesitated, Logan lifted his water for a sip. She could hear the ice rattle as his hand shook ever so slightly. The realization that his self-assurance wasn't as complete as he let on surprised Shani.

"Won't it look a little odd having me working for your company?" she asked. "Once people figure out who I am, the gossip could get ugly."

"Clint's unit is self-contained, a small office off-site in Folsom. Only about a half-dozen employees. I'm sure there'll be some talk—there's no avoiding it. But you've got the bona fides. You're quite qualified for the job."

His praise added icing to an already tempting cake. "Are you ever in that office?" she asked.

"Would you rather I wasn't?"

She'd rather she didn't feel such a confusion of emotions when she was around Logan. "It would make things simpler for me."

If he took offense at her request, she couldn't see it in his face. "I'll schedule meetings when you're not there."

"Then I accept your offer. I know I'll enjoy the work."

He rose abruptly from the table with his plate. "I told Clint you'd start Monday."

She gaped at him. "You didn't even know I'd say yes."

"Is there a problem with starting Monday?"

"I have to give notice."

He scraped the remains of his dinner into the trash. "The university president is an acquaintance of mine. I'm sure the short notice at the library wouldn't be a problem. You can work another weekend at the print shop if necessary. I'll notify Clint that he's to adjust your hours accordingly."

The dinner she'd just eaten sat heavily in her stomach. "This isn't fair."

"What?" He seemed surprised.

"You shouldn't be organizing my life. I have a brain. I can think these things through on my own."

He took her plate, then turned toward the sink. "Can you start work on Monday or not?"

"I'll have to talk to my supervisor at the library. Meanwhile, I don't want you arranging anything with anybody."

He returned to the table and closed the boxes of leftover food. "I'll leave these with you."

She started to rise. "I can help you."

"Don't. I'll do it."

She sat back down. In five silent minutes he had the white boxes in the refrigerator, the dishes in the dishwasher and the table wiped. Finished with the cleanup, Logan headed for the door, then hesitated there as if he had something else to say. His jaw worked as he looked her way. She didn't know if he was considering an apology or wanted to vent the anger that seemed to be brewing inside him.

In the end, he walked out without a word, leaving Shani grappling with the aftermath of a whirlwind.

* * *

As he strode from the cottage, Logan felt too agitated to return to the house. Instead, he circled behind it to the thick cover of trees in the rear. He stopped beside a mammoth oak, its first stout branch a dozen feet up—the perfect place to tie a rope swing. When he'd first visited the house and checked out the forested acreage in the rear, the tree had been like a fantasy from his youth. He could see the swing, could imagine his son or daughter playing there.

Now he leaned against the black oak, his expensive dress shoes crunching in the leaves at his feet, the rough bark scratchy through the thin fabric of his shirt. The Indian summer warmth of mid-October had chilled with the sunset, the night air raising gooseflesh as it brushed against his bare arms. He welcomed the coolness, wished it was colder still. Snow, an impossibility in the Sacramento area in October, would be welcome right about now.

He'd behaved like an ass with Shani, all but telling her what she would and would not do, as if she didn't have a mind to think for herself. That had been his father's modus operandi, treating women as if they were brainless pieces of furniture. Colin Rafferty had liked them pretty, compliant and uncomplaining.

Logan had sworn he'd never be like dear old Dad. And yet he'd married Arianna, a woman so compliant that at times he'd wanted to take her by the shoulders and shake some spine into her. Whatever he gave her, whether it was a night out with him or jewelry or this house, she professed it to be perfect, exactly what she wanted. Except nothing he gave her had ever seemed to make her happy.

Shani was anything but compliant. He doubted she'd

leave him guessing as to what she wanted as he'd so often had to do with Arianna. If he hadn't made sure the job he'd offered Shani was irresistible, that it fit her to a T, she would have turned him down. If he gave her a gift for her birthday, he'd better make sure he knew exactly what she liked and didn't like. Just as he would if he touched her, if he made love to her.

Pushing off from the tree to wander through his backyard forest, he drove that notion from his mind. He'd tried to steer clear of Shani these past several days, to give himself a chance to break the cycle of fantasies he'd fallen into. But while he could school his conscious mind to stop thinking of the way she would feel under his hands, the sounds she would make if he stroked her, dreams were another matter entirely. During the night, there was no bridling his unconscious mind's creativity.

During his marriage, he'd never looked twice at another woman, Shani included. Sex with Arianna had been satisfying but not spectacular; nevertheless, he would have never betrayed his wife. Physical relationships with women had been few and far between since Arianna's death, first because of the grief and guilt, later because he'd let himself get caught up with work to sidestep the urges.

The length of time since he'd been with a woman had to be why Shani intrigued him so. She was living in such close proximity, and she'd engaged in the exquisitely intimate act of carrying his babies. It made sense that the line between reality and sexual fantasy had become so muddled in his mind.

He could see the back of the cottage from his vantage point near the fence line of his property. The bedroom lights were on and he could see a faint shadow crossing the windows as she passed. Despite his better judgment, he imagined her readying for bed, undressing, pulling on that shapeless T-shirt he'd seen her wearing that day in her apartment.

Except that apparently hadn't been her usual sleepwear. In the few weeks Shani had been living at the cottage, Mrs. Singh had been doing her laundry. He'd seen the piles separated out in the laundry room, had seen the colorful bits of nothing Mrs. Singh had put aside for the gentle cycle. Just picturing Shani in those scraps of lace and satin had let loose a torrent of X-rated images.

Feeling like a pervert, Logan continued on, circling around the cottage and heading back toward the house. He'd brought home a pile of reading—a policy manual from his information security officer, a spreadsheet of recommendations for Christmas bonuses, a prospectus for a possible acquisition. Deadly dull, dry work. Just the thing to keep his mind on the straight and narrow.

Yet, later as he slogged through the pages of hi-tech mumbo jumbo, struggling to keep his eyes open and his mind alert, Shani's face kept dancing in his mind's eye. Her soft smile, that lock of hair that he'd smoothed on her head, the imagined come-hither look in her light brown eyes made it impossible to focus.

In the end, he tossed the policy manual across the room in frustration and stomped upstairs to take a long, cold shower.

Chapter Five

After their argument the night of his job offer, Shani and Logan went back to seeing each other only in passing. It should have made her happy that he kept himself absent from her life. But she'd enjoyed at least part of their time together that night, had appreciated getting to know a little bit more about him.

She saw far more of the nurse Logan had hired to administer the injections Shani would continue through her first trimester. Logan was gone by the time Shani left her house in the morning, and at night, it was seven-thirty or eight before he pulled into the driveway. She thought he might turn toward the cottage before walking into the house, but he never even looked her way.

It made no sense that she should feel lonely. They'd agreed their relationship wouldn't extend beyond the surrogacy agreement. But with the long road they still had ahead of them with the pregnancy, it only seemed right they should find a way to get along.

She'd been able to end her commitment to the library and the print shop without a problem. The parting in both cases was so amicable, Shani almost wondered if Logan had intervened after all. She had to remind herself she wasn't indispensable at either job. There were doubtless several other students ready and willing to take her place.

After spending her first day at MiniSport, as the small R and D unit was known, filling out forms, reporting for a required physical exam and sitting through an hour of employee orientation, she was looking forward to some real work on her second day. But when she arrived Tuesday, she found a stack of documents on her desk and a note from Clint asking her to read them to familiarize herself with what the unit was working on.

She did her best, slogging through the dry material, all the while keeping one eye on the clock. She had an eleven-thirty appointment for her first ultrasound and she'd been on pins and needles in anticipation of her first view of the babies-to-be.

She would have thought Logan would want to be there. She'd sent him an e-mail, apprising him of the time, but he hadn't replied as of this morning. Dr. Conners would no doubt be printing out hard copies of the ultrasound images. Shani could just take those up to the house for him to see.

But he ought to be there, to experience firsthand the excitement of seeing his progeny for the first time. Maybe he'd forgotten; she'd call him, remind him of the time. But when she dialed the number she found in the company directory, his administrative assistant said he was out of the office.

As a last-ditch effort, she sent him an e-mail. Then just before she shut down her computer at eleven, she found Logan's reply amidst the junk mail and new-employee notifications from human resources. Short and sweet, it said only, *Meet you at the clinic for the ultrasound.*

He was there waiting for her when she arrived, pacing in front of the clinic entrance. When she saw him, an inexplicable spark of joy lit inside her. She didn't understand the emotion, decided it must have something to do with the reminder of the life growing inside her.

"How have you been feeling?" he asked as he walked inside with her.

"Tired sometimes, but I feel great."

They stepped inside and Shani signed in. She settled in a chair with the two other women waiting with their husbands.

Logan remained standing. "I almost didn't come."

She looked up at him in surprise. "I thought you wanted to be involved in this pregnancy."

"I do." He raked his fingers through his hair. "But this is when we found out. That second time, after the pregnancy test was positive. The doctor did the ultrasound and we discovered…"

"Arianna had lost the baby." Her stomach knotted at the thought.

"They did another pregnancy test to be sure." He shook his head. "Arianna took it hard."

"I know," Shani said quietly.

"I keep forgetting. All those years, I never saw you, but you and my wife were still friends." He shoved his hands into the pockets of his slacks. "I'm grateful for that. You, at least, knew how to comfort her."

"I'm sure you tried." It was the polite thing to say. According to Arianna, he'd acted as if the miscarriage had been no big deal.

Yet his edginess, his unwillingness or inability to relax, seemed to tell a different story. She took his hand. "It'll be fine. Believe me, I still feel very pregnant."

His gaze centered on her. "How do you know?"

"The tiredness, the beginnings of morning sickness. Breakfast made me a bit queasy this morning. Then there's the most obvious symptom—" She broke off, not sure just how much she wanted to share with Logan.

"What?" he prodded.

Her cheeks warmed. She lowered her voice, all too aware of the other men and women in the room. "I'm sore." She gestured at her breasts. "And they're bigger."

That had been the only thing Devon had liked about her being pregnant, that her miniscule breasts had swollen in those first few weeks. They'd gotten even bigger as she'd gotten close to delivering the baby. But Devon had been long gone by then.

She couldn't blame Logan when his gaze dropped to her breasts. She'd all but hung a neon light on them. But as his attention lingered there, his blue eyes darkening, she was mortified to feel her nipples tightening. She told herself it was only because she was embarrassed by Logan's scrutiny. But the tingle of awareness she felt low in her body couldn't be attributed to her feeling of awkwardness. Thank God the sweater she'd put on this morning concealed her reaction.

When Dr. Conners's nurse called Shani's name, Logan's focus snapped away from her. Shani followed the nurse to the exam room. Logan would join her in a few minutes.

The nurse handed her a blue paper drape. "Everything off from the waist down, please."

Although she'd been warned that this first ultrasound used an internal probe, heat rose in Shani's cheeks at the thought of being half-naked with Logan in the room. She knew he'd be at the head of the exam table and wouldn't be able to see anything he shouldn't. No doubt his gaze would be fixed on the television monitor mounted on the far wall and not on her. But the crazy stew of emotions inside her just heightened her awareness of the intimacy of the procedure.

Once she'd set aside her skirt, panty hose and panties, Shani levered herself up onto the exam table and carefully adjusted the drape across her legs. She sat back, willing her nerves to settle. A few minutes later, the doctor entered with Logan and set off a jangling all over again.

He glanced first at her face, then at the blue drape covering her legs, then quickly up at the monitor. Color rose in his cheeks and she guessed he felt just as awkward as she did at the situation. She didn't want him to feel that way, didn't want his first view of his babies to be linked with embarrassment.

She remembered what he'd gone through with Arianna, how difficult that must have been for him. Putting aside her own discomfort, she took his hand. "It's fine, Logan. I promise you."

Dr. Conners inserted the probe inside Shani, adjusted the position. "There you go, Dad. Take a look."

At first it was hard to make out anything on the splotchy gray, white and black image. Then the doctor typed on the keyboard and a white arrow appeared, pointing to a rough black oval with a bit of gray-and-white intruding.

"There's your baby," Dr. Conners said.

"Baby, singular?" Logan asked. "Only one?"

"Only one," Dr. Conners said. "But everything looks good so far."

Shani's awkwardness vanished as she stared at the ultrasound image. It was so small, nearly indistinguishable. A rush of emotion filled her as she fixed on that tiny bit of life. The powerful feelings alarmed her. If she felt this strongly about Logan's baby now, when it was barely a speck on an ultrasound monitor, how would she feel later as the fetus grew inside her? She had to shut those emotions down now.

Logan stared at the screen, his expression rapt. "How soon before it starts to look more like a baby?"

"You'll be able to see a little more at the eight-week ultrasound." Dr. Conners pulled out the probe. "I'll be sending home some printed pictures and a video."

Still dazed, Logan left so that Shani could dress. She met up with him again in the waiting room.

She smiled up at him. "I'm so glad you came."

"Come to lunch with me," he said.

"I thought I'd go back to MiniSport, put in another hour before I go to school."

"Please. I just need to…" He looked around the room, as if searching for the right thing to say. "Come to lunch with me."

She couldn't refuse him. "Should I follow you?"

"We'll take my car. I'll bring you back."

They drove into Roseville, to a small Indian restaurant. Shani ordered a mild chicken curry and rice. Logan went for a scorching lamb vindaloo.

"You can relax now," Shani said as their food arrived.

"It's still too early." He nudged the basket of naan bread toward her. "You went through this before, seeing your baby on an ultrasound."

The reminder of her son, even after all these years, hit her like a punch to the stomach. Logan must have seen the reaction in her face because he reached across the table toward her.

"Damn, I'm sorry. I shouldn't have asked."

"It's okay."

"It isn't." He took her hand. "I'm just…hell, I don't know. Seeing the ultrasound…getting past that hurdle…"

"I never had an ultrasound. My insurance wouldn't cover it." She picked at the curry. "It wouldn't have been a good idea, anyway."

She'd thought at the time that seeing the images would just strengthen the attachment toward the baby growing inside her. But it didn't matter. The connection had developed, anyway, day by day. The morning she handed her son off to the representative from the adoption agency, it had felt as if her heart had been torn from her chest.

Logan stroked the back of her hand with his thumb. "I thought it wouldn't mean much to me, seeing it. But it makes it real."

Unwilling to revisit the grief of the past, Shani focused on the path of Logan's thumb along her skin. In that moment, she wished for more than that slight contact, that he would take her in his arms.

It wouldn't have to be Logan, she told herself. Anyone would be just as much a comfort. It was only their shared experience that drew her so intensely to him.

He drew his hand back and took another bite of his vindaloo. "Have you had any contact with him at all?"

"His mother sent me pictures for a few years." Shani forced herself to take a mouthful of chicken and rice. "It was too hard. I asked her to stop." Now she wished she hadn't.

"But you still know where he lives."

Shani shook her head. "They moved. I considered asking my mother if she could find out where, but then I thought it might be better…"

He pushed aside his plate. "I could find him for you."

"No! Please…" She struggled to clear her thoughts. "I don't want to intrude on his life, to complicate things for him."

"If you change your mind, you'll tell me."

She tore off a piece of the flat naan. "Maybe someday." When she felt strong enough. When she could meet him and walk away without a broken heart.

A sudden thought had her lifting her gaze to Logan's. "You wouldn't do it on your own…go searching for him."

A flicker in his face told her it had crossed his mind. "Don't," she told him.

"I'll wait for you to ask," he said, and she heard the conviction in his tone.

Shani managed to eat enough that she couldn't possibly feel guilty about depriving the baby. The drive back to the clinic where her car was parked passed in silence. Logan took a cell call, speaking into his wireless headset as he navigated the streets.

He pulled in beside her car and shut off the engine. Shani put out a hand to stop him. "You don't have to get out."

But when she climbed out, he did, as well, following her around to the driver's side of her Mustang. He stood there as she unlocked the door and opened it.

When she started to climb in, she felt his hand on her shoulder. She looked up to see him gazing down at her, his expression unreadable.

Then his arms were around her, holding her close.

For a moment, she hesitated, his warmth soaking into her, his hands spread across her back. Then she wrapped her arms around him, absorbing his strength. Tears pricked her eyes, her throat tightened, and his comfort washed through her.

When he backed away finally, his gaze dropped to her wet eyes. Gently, he brushed the tears aside with his fingertips. His hand lingered on her cheek.

"Thank you," he said softly. Then he turned on his heel and walked away.

When Shani returned home that evening, she found one of Mrs. Singh's notes taped to her door. *Mr. Rafferty would like you to join him for dinner tonight at seven.*

Wariness warred with a spurt of joy inside her. Exhausted from the day, Shani wasn't sure which would be more difficult—another sparring session with Logan, or grappling with the confusing emotions she experienced when she was with him. She would have simply called Mrs. Singh and begged off, but she suspected that as politely worded as the note was, this was more of a command performance than a request. If she didn't show, Logan might come down here demanding to know why.

It was just after six, and she dithered over whether to use the hour studying her industrial-organization text for tomorrow's test. But such a brief time wouldn't drill into her the concepts she barely understood. She needed a major brain transplant for that, exchanging hers for that of an expert in economics.

In the end, she collapsed into bed for a nap, taking care to set her alarm first to be sure she didn't oversleep. She woke before it went off, which gave her enough time to change from jeans and a turtleneck into a full blue denim skirt and a pale periwinkle V-neck sweater.

She told herself she wasn't dressing up for Logan. She just wanted out of the clothes she'd been wearing all day.

As she walked toward the main house, light glowed from the windows, bright against the near dark. Although the small frame house she grew up in back in Iowa City was nothing like this expansive farmhouse, she felt the ache of homesickness. She hadn't been back to Iowa since spring break, and only for three days. She wouldn't be seeing her mother and sister again until Thanksgiving. That holiday seemed months away.

She'd just reached the porch steps when the front door opened. Logan stepped outside, his usual uniform of slacks, dress shirt and tie replaced by khakis and a polo shirt. The ache of loneliness inside Shani eased as he moved toward her, taking her hand to help her up the last step. The heat of the contact zinged through her, tempting her to lean closer to him.

Thankfully, he let her go to open the door. "Dinner's almost ready," he said as he moved aside to let her enter.

The tiled foyer led immediately into a spacious but homey great room. Comfortable sofas flanked the fireplace, where a pellet stove warmed the room. She could see the open kitchen beyond, where Mrs. Singh worked on the finishing touches for their meal. Through the door to the dining room, Shani glimpsed the table set for two.

A chess set, the pieces laid out ready for a game, sat on the coffee table, a cardboard file box on the floor beside it. In the otherwise tidy room, the box seemed out of place.

When Logan noticed her looking at the box, he slid it under the table out of sight. "Mrs. Singh is ready to serve."

With a hand lightly pressed to the small of her back, he escorted her to the dining room. Mrs. Singh smiled and greeted Shani as she set salads on the table before hurrying back to the kitchen.

The salad, butter lettuce with pears, dried cranberries and candied walnuts, took the edge off Shani's appetite. She nearly inhaled the plateful, and one of the still-warm whole wheat rolls besides.

When she caught Logan staring at her, she flushed. "Sorry. Based on past experience, I seem to be either starving or queasy when I'm pregnant."

"No need to apologize. I'm glad you're able to eat."

"You might not be so glad when I'm big as a house." She'd said it lightly, as a joke, but Logan's expression was serious.

"But the baby will be growing along with you. Arianna hardly gained an ounce."

Shani's heart squeezed tight. A baby was all her friend had wanted. She would have been thrilled to watch her body expanding to accommodate her child.

As Shani herself had been, eight years ago. Except sorrow had counterbalanced that joy. She could never allow herself to feel happy without reminding herself she was one day closer to the moment she would give up her son.

Shani pushed aside the memories. "Was there something else you wanted to talk about tonight? A reason you invited me to dinner?"

He tore apart a roll, the tendons on the backs of his hands taut. "Can't I just invite you?"

"I don't understand what our relationship is supposed to be. We're not friends…we don't seem to like each other enough for that. And I refuse to consider this surrogacy a business arrangement. So why are we here together?"

He set the roll on his bread plate. "I've told you before, I want to be part of this pregnancy. To do that, I have no choice but to be with you."

The way he said it, it sounded to Shani as if spending

time with her was the last thing he wanted to do. The thought stung. "In that case, I agree. We'll need to see more of each other."

"Dinners together make the most sense. I won't obligate you every night, can't promise myself due to my own commitments. But if you're not otherwise occupied, I want you here for dinner."

It wasn't an unreasonable request, but Shani chafed at Logan telling her what to do. "Sometimes I'm tired in the evenings when I get home from school. Too tired to want to come over here."

"Then I'll have Mrs. Singh bring dinner to the cottage. We'll eat together there, catch up on what's happening with you. It won't take more than an hour."

Even an hour with Logan could be exhausting by itself. Still, she told him, "I suppose that would work."

Mrs. Singh came in to clear the salad, then a few moments later brought them plates of beef bourguignonne. With the tumble of confusion inside her, Shani thought she wouldn't be able to eat another bite. But the savory fragrance of beef and mushrooms overruled her emotions.

"There was another reason I asked you over tonight. Beyond the issue of keeping tabs on the progress of your pregnancy." Logan held the basket of rolls out to her. "That box in the great room—I wanted to give it to you."

"What's in it?"

"Some of Arianna's things. A necklace, some other odds and ends she'd collected over the years." He stabbed a piece of beef, swirled it in the rich sauce. "And her diary."

Chapter Six

The moment he told her about the file box in the great room, Logan could see Shani was eager to look through it. She finished her dinner quickly, then waited with thinly disguised impatience as he took his last few bites.

"Go ahead," he told her, picking up the plates to take to Mrs. Singh. "I'll be there in a minute."

But when he set the dishes on the kitchen counter, he couldn't bring himself to immediately join Shani. Instead, he found a vantage point just inside the kitchen where he could watch her, to see her reaction when she opened the box.

He'd kept the file box in a corner of the walk-in closet in his bedroom for the year Arianna had been gone. It contained the handful of things he could neither give away nor leave on display as a remembrance of her. The items in that cardboard box each had a significance to Arianna, a specialness he didn't always understand. It had seemed best to simply store them out of sight, perhaps for a day when he would be able to make a better decision as to their disposition.

Most of the rest of Arianna's things, he'd given away to charity—her clothes and shoes, her books, a collection of unicorns she'd kept in her sitting room. Then there was the handful of belongings he'd arranged to have sent to Shani—a few pieces of jewelry, the childhood portrait, a silver brush-and-comb set—which Arianna had specifically mentioned during their discussion about settling her affairs and the disposition of the embryos if something happened to her.

Only after he'd disposed of the rest of Arianna's personal effects had it occurred to him he should have called Shani, to let her go through Arianna's things, to see if there was anything she wanted. He was glad he'd at least thought to offer her these last few mementos. It seemed such a paltry gift compared to what she was giving him—his child.

Shani had the lid off the box, but still hadn't yet taken anything out. He could see from where he stood just inside the entry to the kitchen the mix of emotions on her face, the barest glint of tears in her eyes. Seeing her on the edge of crying hit him as hard now as it had earlier. He'd failed so many times to comfort Arianna; he couldn't just leave Shani to deal with the grief alone.

He headed out into the great room and sat beside Shani on the sofa, a hand on her back. Touching her was problematic; his body responded to her no matter how much he told himself he was out of line. But he could ignore the X-rated messages his body was feeding his brain. He wasn't a damn teenager.

Shani had pulled out a silver chain with a silver-and-amethyst unicorn pendant. She cradled the necklace in the palm of her hand as if it was the most precious treasure in the world.

"I gave this to her," Shani said, her voice husky from emotion. "On her thirtieth birthday."

He remembered seeing it around Arianna's neck one day, had complimented her on how nice it looked on her. She'd smiled, said thank you, but didn't mention its source. Maybe because she knew about the friction between him and Shani. Maybe because she so obviously preferred it to the expensive gold-and-diamond earrings he'd given her that year.

"She loved that necklace," Logan told Shani. "She wore it all the time."

Taking in a deep breath, Shani glanced over at him with a wobbly smile. "She'd wear it when we were together, but I thought she was just being polite. Sometimes it was hard to know what was going on inside her head."

That surprised him. "I thought you two talked about everything."

"We did. But she kept secrets, even from me."

He'd thought he was the only one Arianna hid herself from. That she held back from the one friend she'd allowed so deeply into her life astounded him.

Shani removed three small tissue-wrapped bundles and peeled away the paper. She set aside the glass paperweight swirled with vivid jewel colors, then smiled in turn at the cat carved from blue stone and the pewter dragon on a quartz pedestal.

"Did you give her those?" Logan asked.

Shani shook her head. "We'd go to craft fairs sometimes on Saturdays. She bought the cat and dragon there. You should recognize this, though." She held out the paperweight.

"I know she kept it on her desk." He took it from Shani, the smooth glass orb cool against his skin.

"You bought this for her. Not long after you married, according to what Arianna told me."

With the heavy glass resting in his palm, the memory returned. He'd found it on a trip to Ohio. He'd spent the morning with a venture capitalist interested in investing in Good Sport and had been certain the visit had gone badly. It hadn't—that infusion of cash kept the company afloat another year. On his way back to the hotel, he'd happened upon the glassworks, and had gone into their gift shop. The glass orb, with its tangle of color inside, had reminded him of Arianna.

"It surprises me that she told you about this. I thought she didn't like it. She kept it hidden away on her desk."

"It was the one thing you'd given her out of the blue, for no reason. That meant a lot to her."

Unexpected gifts—if only it had been as simple as that to make his late wife happy. But he suspected he would have found a way to give her the wrong gift.

Only the diary remained in the box. Shani lifted the leather-bound volume out and set it on her lap. "Did you know she kept a diary?"

"She started it a couple of years before she died. The few times I caught her writing in it, she'd put it away the moment she saw me."

Shani tugged lightly at the strap holding the diary shut. "It's locked. Do you have the key?"

"I don't know where she kept the key. It would be easy enough to break the lock or cut the strap."

"No." Shani hugged the book to her chest. "That

wouldn't be right. I'm not even sure I should be reading it."

"I emptied her desk, but I can look through it again for the key, if you want."

"I'd appreciate that." She set the diary back in the box, then rewrapped the cat and dragon. "You should keep the paperweight."

It sat heavily in his hand, far beyond the few ounces it weighed. He secured the tissue paper around it and returned it to the box.

Shani's arm pressed against his as she replaced the cat and dragon figures. She picked up the necklace, cupping it in her palm.

He took it from her. "Let me put it on you."

It was a foolhardy move. The noise in the kitchen had quieted, which meant Mrs. Singh had gone to her room for the night. He and Shani were essentially alone here, nothing but his own self-control to keep him from doing something stupid.

Undoing the clasp, he parted the chain and brought it around the back of Shani's neck. He couldn't help but touch her now. As his fingers fumbled with the slide on the clasp, his hand brushed the tender nape of her neck again and again. Her skin seemed hotter with each point of contact.

When he finally got the slide open and fastened the clasp, he released the chain. But he couldn't seem to pull away. His hands settled on the soft wool of her sweater, his thumbs along either side of her neck. With her head bowed, there was an inch of bare skin between where her hair ended and the neckline of her sweater. Just enough room to press a kiss.

He would have pulled his hands away, would have risen to his feet and out of temptation's reach, but for one small sound. Shani's soft sigh, her breath catching as she released it. Then she shifted, not away from him, but closer, increasing the contact of his hands.

When he lowered his mouth to her soft skin, stroked it along the curve where her neck and shoulder met, she sighed again and tipped her head back. He trailed kisses along the slender column of her throat, to the angle of her jaw, then the lobe of her ear. He touched that tender lobe with just the tip of his tongue, the briefest contact before he drew away again. Her breathy moan sent sensations shooting to the base of his spine.

"Logan."

He could barely hear his name falling from her lips. He hesitated, thinking she might want him to stop, but she leaned closer again, her hand falling lightly on his thigh. Each fingertip seemed to burn through the fabric of his khakis to the heated skin beneath. His flesh, already hard and aching, seemed to swell even more at her touch.

She turned her face toward him, angling her mouth toward his. He gave in to the urge he had ignored since that first day he'd seen her in his office. He brushed his lips against hers. Her mouth was even warmer, even softer than he'd imagined. He wanted desperately to dive inside, to taste the sweetness within.

The slightest tension in Shani's shoulders, a faint hesitation, brought him back to sudden sanity. He drew back, his mouth still moist from hers. Her eyes opened and she stared up at him, looking as stunned as he felt. Then she jumped to her feet, stumbling against the coffee table as she backed away.

"I should go back to the cottage." Her hands shook as she put the lid on the file box. "I need to get into work early tomorrow."

Logan rose, feeling like an idiot, appalled at the way

he'd touched Shani, kissed her. He ought to apologize, say something, but she wouldn't even look at him.

She wrapped her arms around the lightweight box and picked it up, holding it in front of her like a shield. "Thank you for the…for dinner. For giving me Arianna's things."

He followed her to the door, but she still wouldn't look at him. "I'll see you for dinner tomorrow night," he said as he opened the door for her. "As we agreed."

She nodded and slipped out. He followed her onto the porch. "I'll walk you to the cottage."

"No!" Hooking the box under one arm, she hurried down the steps. "It's only a few feet. I'm fine."

She was right, of course. He could clearly see the gravel path between here and the small guesthouse. Outdoor lights illuminated the way. He could keep an eye on her until she was safely inside.

But he wanted to be with her. Wanted to walk close enough beside her that he could feel her warmth, take in her scent, hear the sound of her breathing. Completely wrong, completely inappropriate, but his awareness of her had somehow invaded him to his core. It was difficult to think of anything else.

But he stayed on the porch, followed her every step to her door, raised his hand to answer her wave just before she disappeared inside the cottage. Then he returned to his own lonely house, with traces of Shani lingering everywhere.

For the next few weeks, as Shani worked in the mornings at MiniSport, and during her classes, memories of Logan's kiss persisted, almost as real as the act itself. The tantalizing images that danced in her mind were the worst in the evenings when she shared her dinner with

Logan, when the subject of her fantasies sat across from her at the cottage's small kitchen table. But her body reacted to him even when he wasn't there, when the smallest thought of him flitted into her consciousness.

And when they shared dinner, Logan's presence seemed to charge the small cottage with electricity, sharpening Shani's hunger, intensifying the taste of the food on her plate. At the same time, she could barely remember what she ate, if it had been meat or fish or chicken, one of Mrs. Singh's Indian specialties or an ordinary hamburger.

The second ultrasound at the eight-week mark further reassured Shani and Logan that the baby was developing well, that they could soon consider the pregnancy an ordinary one. As ordinary as the unusual arrangement could be.

Temptation to open Arianna's diary had been difficult to resist since she brought it to the cottage. It was more than simple curiosity. Shani wanted to know if Arianna had felt the same when she'd kissed her husband, if she'd found his mere presence as distracting as Shani did.

Arianna hadn't shared any of the intimate details of her marriage with Shani. But maybe she wrote about them in the diary. Maybe somewhere Arianna noted that in spite of Logan's sometimes cold demeanor, women who spent time with him found him irresistible. That the emotions Shani was experiencing were simple lust and nothing more.

When she'd found herself weakening, reconsidering her vow to open the diary only if she located the key, she removed the leather book from her nightstand drawer. After considering and rejecting several options for where to hide it, she stuffed the diary between the mattress and box springs, underneath the bedskirt.

On the Monday of Shani's fourth week of employment at MiniSport, after enduring her usual morning injections, she watched for Logan's departure before heading out to work herself. First thing in the morning, she seemed to have fewer defenses against Logan, so she didn't want to chance confronting him. She'd be seeing him later, anyway; the MiniSport team would be convening at Good Sport for an all-hands lunch.

She'd come to love her job at MiniSport, so much so that she wondered if it would be possible to continue working there after graduation. But she found it difficult to focus on her work with the prospect of seeing Logan at lunchtime looming over her, even though the setting would be a crowded meeting on employee benefit changes.

So far, no one knew about Logan's arrangement with her. At eight weeks, she'd only put on a few pounds. Even the most discerning would never guess she was pregnant. Still, Shani feared that someone would somehow divine the connection between her and Logan, would see something in the way Shani looked at him. Would see something in her face, in her eyes, that would give away her secret.

Eventually, her pregnancy would show. She and Logan had agreed they would reveal the truth as needed. First, she'd simply let people know that she was acting as a gestational carrier. Later they could announce the child was Logan's.

Since she had to go directly from the luncheon at Good Sport to Sac State, Shani had to take her own car rather than carpool as a few of the others were doing. They left in a laughing group while she stayed behind to put a few finishing touches on a spreadsheet. After ten minutes, she headed out to the parking lot.

As she waited to pull into traffic, she was surprised to see a familiar car stopped in the next driveway down. The owner of the dark green Nissan sedan apparently lived in Logan's neighborhood and worked somewhere in Folsom. She'd first seen the car a couple of weeks ago and noticed it traced the same path to work as hers. Since then, she'd seen the car three or four times. Sometimes she had the feeling it was following her, but whenever she reached MiniSport, the sedan continued on, no doubt to one of the myriad office buildings along East Bidwell.

The car had stopped well back from the street. Was the driver waiting for someone to exit the building next door? She tried to catch a glimpse of the driver's face, but suddenly, he gunned the car's engine, then veered up Bidwell with a screech of tires.

In a hurry for his own lunchtime appointment, no doubt, tamping down her unease. Shani made her way through the heavy flow of cars, wending her way along the surface streets toward the Good Sport headquarters. Between the traffic and a few unfortunate red lights, Shani was five minutes late.

Set up amphitheater style, each of the two-hundred-plus seats with a pull-up desk, Good Sport's large conference facility was packed. Stepping inside, Shani tried to see through the milling bodies, searching in vain for an empty seat. As she scanned the noisy room, she lingered on the face of each tall, dark-haired man, instinctively seeking out Logan. But if he was here, she couldn't find him in the mass of people.

Just as she'd resigned herself to standing in the back, she spotted a friendly face. Marilyn, a Web designer on the MiniSport team, waved to Shani from the far end of the fifth row, gesturing beside her to what had to be a vacant seat. Shani threaded her way through the crowd, smiling and greeting the few other employees she recognized.

Once she'd made her way to the other end of the fifth row, Shani saw two empty places beside Marilyn. As Shani picked up the thick notebook on the seat next to Marilyn, she spied an index card in the aisle seat with *reserved* written across it. "Is the other for Clint?"

Marilyn pointed across the room. "He's sitting over there with a couple of the other managers. He asked me to save this one for you."

A woman Shani recognized from Human Resources shouted above the din for everyone to take their seats. With employees settling into their places, Shani finally had a clear view of the front of the room. In a cluster of a half-dozen men and women in business suits with visitor badges clipped to their lapels, Logan stood with his back to her.

Her breath caught at the sight of him, as if she hadn't eaten dinner with him last night, hadn't watched him drive away just that morning. The kiss they'd shared might as well have been yesterday instead of weeks ago. Her mouth still tingled from the memory, the flesh along the back of her neck warmed as if his breath curled there.

Whether he turned because he'd finished his discussion with the visitors or he sensed her focus on him, she didn't know. She only prayed he couldn't somehow detect the thoughts rampaging through her mind.

When he moved toward her, every nerve in her body seemed to fire at once. She had to will herself to remain in her seat instead of jumping to her feet and running from the room.

He picked up the fat black notebook on the seat beside her. "How are you?" he asked.

"That seat's reserved," she said, barely mustering the breath to speak.

"For me," he told her.

Of course it was. "I think it would be better if we didn't sit together."

"It would."

He pulled the desk up over his lap and set the black notebook on it. As the cluster of visitors assembled on the stage below, he leaned close enough for only Shani to hear his murmured words. "I had to be with you, anyway."

His bald statement sent heat shooting through her. Then he shifted, bringing his knee within millimeters of her thigh. To an onlooker, it would seem innocuous. Logan had only needed to stretch out his long legs to get comfortable.

But to Shani, it was as if he'd claimed her by intruding ever so slightly into her space. She could ask him to move away, would have if it had been another man. But with Logan, she wanted to get closer, to touch him, to feel him skin to skin. Just as she had after that dinner two weeks ago.

The speaker seemed to drone on, incomprehensible to Shani's overheated mind. Her world centered on an invisible thread of connection between her and Logan. Everyone else in the room might as well have vanished.

When the benefits presentation finally concluded, Logan slipped from the row to go speak with the visitors. Shani rose, relieved she wouldn't have to squeeze past him to escape. Logan's spell on her lingered, but her mind cleared enough that she could smile at Marilyn and say her goodbyes.

Just as she reached the door, about to make her escape, a hand brushed her shoulder. Logan's voice rumbled in her ear. "I'll see you tonight for dinner?"

She moved aside so that others could exit. "Yes. Of course."

"I've made a reservation for seven o'clock at Il Paradiso." He spoke softly, his expression neutral, no doubt to give the appearance of a businesslike conversation between them.

She didn't know what would be worse—going out to dinner when she was tired from a long day or sharing the meal in the more intimate setting of his home or the cottage. She wanted to run away from him; she wanted to bring him closer.

"If you change it to seven-thirty, I could get a short nap in." At least then she'd have more energy to resist the urgings of her overactive imagination.

"I'll pick you up at seven, then." He turned on his heel and walked away.

She walked to her car in a daze, wondering how she would absorb anything in her lectures today. She had to get her mind back on track. Considering the mire she was already in with her industrial organization class, it was imperative she give her afternoon classes her full attention.

It wasn't until she was in her car, waiting to pull out into traffic, that she saw the dark green sedan parked in a far corner of the Good Sport lot. She wouldn't have noticed it at all, except that it was backing from its parking space just as she passed the row.

It drove slowly along the aisle toward Shani, then stopped halfway down. Although traffic had cleared, Shani waited, looking back at the car, a prickling along her skin.

Movement caught her eye as a white minivan backed from its parking space between Shani and the green sedan. With a squeal of tires, the Nissan backed up, veered into the nearest lane, turned around and made a quick exit.

Shani hesitated long enough for the minivan's driver to honk at her before she headed out herself and made her way to campus.

Chapter Seven

After disrupting Logan's entire afternoon, it looked as if Shani would unsettle his evening as well. At seven-thirty-five, she had yet to make her appearance at Il Paradiso.

It was his own fault. He'd been tied up with a call to his manufacturing plant in Mumbai with no hope of getting home in time to pick Shani up at seven. He'd called her at six-thirty and they'd arranged to meet at the restaurant at the appointed time. He could tell from her sleepy, liquid voice that he'd woken her from her nap, and desire had shot through him as he imagined her warm under the covers.

Even now, the image had the power to drive heat through him. Logan lifted his glass of merlot and took a sip, hoping to douse the fire. But the fine wine couldn't banish Shani from his awareness any more than work had since they parted company after the all-hands meeting.

Logan had chosen Il Paradiso because he knew the

owners, Vince and Charlotte Anzalone, and because it was a place he conducted many of his business deals. He'd had some lunatic idea that he would be better able to behave himself here, at this watering hole for movers and shakers in the Sacramento area, than he could in Shani's cottage.

But he'd forgotten Il Paradiso's subdued lighting, the way the table layout and strategically placed greenery provided intimate niches for each customer. In the corner booth in which he'd been seated, he could kiss Shani, press her back against the soft leather and no one would be the wiser.

Damn. He shook his head to cast off his wayward thoughts, then checked his watch again. Seven-forty. Where was she?

Logan fumbled in his jacket pocket for his cell phone. Before he could dial, he caught a glimpse of Shani through Il Paradiso's glass front doors. Then she stepped inside and all coherent thought vanished from his mind.

A dress the color of merlot shimmered on her body, clinging to her still-slender curves, spaghetti straps glittering with rhinestones. The full, flowing skirt barely cleared her knee, and the bodice covered her small breasts modestly, but every inch of visible skin glowed golden, begging for a man's touch.

The waiter, Trent, pointed her toward Logan's table and she started through the dining room, every man in the place tracking her graceful progress. A state assemblyman sharing dinner with a lobbyist knocked over his water glass as she passed him; the CEO of a local tech firm jumped when his wife kicked him under the table for staring.

Logan rose to seat her, glad of the excuse to take her hand and ease her into the booth. Even Trent, who should have been as unmoved by Shani as he would by any woman, couldn't seem to stop grinning as he hurried over to lay a napkin in Shani's lap.

A surge of possessiveness took hold of Logan as he slid around next to her. Every man in the room was gasping with envy, but this woman was with *him*. Even as he realized how wrong that feeling was, even as he tried to suppress it, every cell in his body felt more alive now that Shani was here.

He grappled with his empty mind, trying to remember what he'd wanted to discuss with her tonight. "You're late," he finally said, at a loss to say anything else.

She reached for her water glass, Arianna's silver unicorn necklace catching the light as Shani leaned forward. "I fell asleep again after you called and only woke up about thirty minutes ago. The first dress I pulled out of the closet wouldn't zip up past my waist." She looked around the room, a trace of worry on her face. "I hope this one is okay."

He nearly laughed. The only problem was that Charlotte would be ticked when none of her male customers ate another bite due to the distraction Shani caused. "It's fine," he told her, a monumental understatement.

The kitchen door swung open and Charlotte zigzagged through the room with the salads Logan had ordered. Vince was right behind her with the pepper grinder, as if they didn't have Trent and two other waiters to do the job.

Charlotte set the Caesar salads down and Vince wielded the two-foot-tall pepper grinder. Logan knew if he didn't introduce them to Shani, the two would linger by the table until dessert was served.

"This is Shani Jacoby," he told them. "She was a longtime friend of Arianna's."

That was enough to satisfy Vince, but Logan could still see the speculative look in Charlotte's eyes. He knew the Anzalones well enough and could have told them the rest—about the surrogacy, the fact that Shani was staying at his estate. But the same possessiveness flared up. Just as he wanted Shani to himself, he wanted the news of her pregnancy to remain private for the moment.

When Charlotte and Vince returned to the kitchen, Logan brought the conversation around to what he needed to discuss with her. "I have a favor to ask."

He saw the wariness in her gaze. "A favor?"

"There's a dinner on Saturday, a charity event. I'd planned to go alone, but one of the guests at my table had to back out. I'd like you to come with me."

"I'm going to be busy this weekend."

Jealousy burned a hole in his stomach. "You have a date?"

"No." She reached for another roll and set it on her plate. "I'll be working on an extra-credit project for my industrial organization class."

"You have to take a break for dinner."

"I don't know if I can."

For the first time, he heard the distress in her voice. All those years married to Arianna, he at least could discern when a woman was unhappy. Whether he could do any more for Shani than he'd been able to do for his late wife was another matter.

"What's going on, Shani? What's the matter?"

She shook her head, as if unwilling to answer. "Tell me," he prodded.

Her confession spilled out. "I'm nearly failing the class. The extra-credit project has to make up for the dismal grade I got on the midterm."

Relief flooded Logan. This was something he could help her with. "You should have told me."

Her head hanging, she tore apart her roll. "I kept hoping a light bulb would come on and I'd magically understand it all."

Fingers pressing lightly against her cheek, Logan turned her to face him. "You should have asked me for help. I have an MBA, I'm CEO of an international company. I think I might know a little bit about industrial organization."

She shook her head, dislodging his hand. "I can handle this on my own."

"The hell you can. Not if you don't understand the material. It makes no sense to keep beating your head against the wall."

"I have to stand on my own two feet." She tipped her chin up, but the tears glinting in her eyes told him that despite her brave words, she was groping for a lifeline.

"Who told you that?" he asked. "Your mother? Your long-lost father?"

She wouldn't meet his gaze. "No one had to tell me."

A sudden flash of insight supplied the answer. "It was the bastard that fathered your baby, wasn't it? Right before he walked out and left you to deal with your pregnancy alone."

Now her light brown eyes flashed with anger. "That isn't any of your business."

"I say it is. You're pregnant with my child. I want you in top physical condition to give my baby its best chance of continuing to term. If you're running yourself ragged in your classes, stressing yourself out because you're too proud to ask for assistance, I'm stepping in."

She held herself stiffly, tension clear in her face. "I

can handle this on my own," she said again, but there was little conviction in the soft-spoken declaration.

He pushed on. "We'll have our dinners early the next four nights. We'll go through your textbook, clarify any concepts you don't understand. I'll schedule my weekend so I'm available to answer questions while you're working on the extra-credit project."

Even as he laid out his intentions, he realized the one flaw in his plan. He would be extending the time he spent with her beyond the hour or so they shared at dinner. The longer the time they spent together, the greater the temptation, the greater the test of his ability to resist touching her, kissing her again.

She fixed her gaze on him and for a moment, he wondered if she could read what was in his mind. "I don't want you taking over every corner of my life. There has to be some part of me I can keep to myself."

Every part of her seemed like a mystery to him. And he felt as if he was the one under her control. "Then consider it part of your job training. Consider it quid pro quo for attending the fund-raiser with me and filling out my table. But I'm not letting you fail the damn class out of stubbornness."

Shani's eyes narrowed, anger flashing in them, but Trent's arrival at the table with their food derailed whatever she intended to say. She ate her linguine with white clam sauce in silence, but he could sense the explosion simmering under the surface.

Shani tamped down her ire with an effort, the cascading emotions within her tying her stomach up in knots. But she forced herself to eat at least half the plate of pasta the waiter had brought. She loved linguine with white clam sauce, but the fact that Logan had ordered it for her without asking her preference was just further proof of his domination of her every waking moment.

She waved off the cannoli that arrived shortly after the waiter cleared the plates. Uncanny that he'd picked her favorites—she adored the crunchy pastry stuffed with sweetened ricotta. But as unsettled as she felt, she didn't dare take even a taste of such a sensual delight.

She waited until the waiter had brought Logan's coffee and left them alone again. "I'll accept your help. I'll attend the fund-raiser with you." She took a breath. "But you can't touch me anymore. You can't…kiss me."

He didn't so much as move a millimeter closer to her, but his gaze flickered ever so briefly to her mouth. A kernel of heat burned deep within Shani in response.

He nodded. "Agreed."

"In seven months, once your baby is born, we part company. We won't have any further connection with each other." She ignored the ache that settled around her heart.

His bland expression gave away nothing of how he felt about her pronouncement. She doubted it mattered to him one way or another. "You're under no obligation to me after the baby is born."

Despair filled her at the reminder. She'd known it all along, had told herself as much every day. This life growing inside her was never meant to be hers. She was only a vessel. And unlike her own son, there was not even a genetic link with the tiny being growing within her.

She was just tired, worried about school, on edge because of her persistent attraction to Logan. That and hormones had thrown her emotions out of whack. With a good night's sleep she'd be able to put the situation back into perspective.

Once Logan had finished his dessert and coffee, he paid the check, then walked her to her car. She would

have just as soon sat there for a few minutes to gather
her thoughts, to try to find a balance for herself after the
turmoil of the past hour, but she could see Logan's
Mercedes near the exit, waiting. No point in signaling
him to go; even if he could have seen her wave in the
dark, she doubted he would leave.

So she pulled in behind him and followed the tail-
lights of the Mercedes back to Logan's. Once they
reached the private road that led to the estate, Shani
flipped up her rearview mirror to avoid the glare of
headlights from a car that was behind her. After Logan
made his left into the drive, Shani had to wait for an
oncoming truck to pass before she could turn.

Logan's gate had shut before she reached it and she
had to enter the code again. While she waited for the
gate to open, she noticed the car following her was still
there. She edged forward, although she knew she was
clear of the street and that the dark sedan should be able
to pass. But it didn't move.

Fear trickled through her, urging her to punch the ac-
celerator and get through the now-open gate. But anger
welled up in the wake of fear, and she wrenched open
the car door. She hurried toward the sedan, shouting out,
"Who are you? What do you want?"

The car took off before she could see the driver,
before she could even be certain it was the same dark
green Nissan. It wasn't until it had gotten well down the
road that it occurred to her she should have noted the
license plate number. But for all she knew, it was
someone lost on the confusing, twisting roads of
Logan's neighborhood, and the crazy lady jumping from
her car had frightened them.

She had to enter the code a second time to open the
gate, and by then Logan had walked back down the

drive looking for her. She stopped and opened her car window. "I'm fine," she told him to forestall a grilling. "Just had a little trouble with the gate code."

He leaned down, his blue eyes scanning her face as if checking for trouble. "I'll call the company out tomorrow to inspect it."

"Don't bother. It was my error." Tiredness weighed on her. "I've got to get to bed."

He backed away and she rolled up the window. But where she should have felt relieved to drive away, to be left to herself, a trace of fear still lingered. As unwise as it seemed, a part of her wished he would follow her to the cottage and stay there with her, keeping her safe.

By Friday night, the glimmer of hope Shani had felt after her first study session with Logan had blossomed into complete confidence that she could not only do a good job with the extra-credit assignment, she could pass the upcoming final, as well. Her understanding of perfect and monopolistic competition and price discrimination might not win her a Nobel prize in economics, but the concepts were no longer the overwhelming monsters they had been.

And she'd made it through the week's tutorials without one stray touch, without one forbidden kiss. Not that her imagination hadn't filled in for what hadn't happened, teasing her with fantasies after she went to bed each night, crowding her dreams with erotic images. But she'd been able to keep those sizzling scenes out of real life.

Now, as they settled in Logan's living room for another after-dinner session, Shani flipped open her notebook to a fresh page. "I know you've explained this before, but I'm still not getting it. How do you define the 'Prisoner's Dilemma' as it applies to collusion?"

He stretched his long legs out on the coffee table beside her. "We have to go back to oligopolistic market structures."

Her eyes glazed over. "Why is nothing in economics in plain English?"

"Let's take a step back." He reached across her for the textbook. "The short version of the Prisoner's Dilemma is that you have a situation where two individuals would prosper as a whole if they cooperated, but even more individually if they cheat." Flipping through the book, he found the pertinent page.

Shani scanned the text he pointed to. "Right. Two prisoners will most likely rat each other out rather than stay quiet and risk their buddy ratting them out."

Logan then explained—again—how the Prisoner's Dilemma related to economic markets. He neither spoke down to her nor went over her head and managed to make the arcane subject fascinating.

She scribbled down notes as fast as she could, patting herself on the back that they'd spent the better part of an hour together without her mind straying once into illicit territory. Then she made the mistake of looking up at him to ask a question about product differentiation.

The intensity in his blue gaze as he met hers stole her breath and sent heat shimmering up her spine. The air was charged between them, almost as palpable as Logan's touch. Every resolution she'd sworn to herself evaporated in the wake of that sizzling visual connection.

She shook her head, slowly, to warn him off. Even though that was the last thing she wanted from him. She put a hand up to stop him as he leaned closer. But it somehow landed on his chest, and her fingers curled into the soft knit of his polo shirt.

She knew it would take only the slightest effort to push him back. But his warm palm had curved against her cheek, tipping back her head. And his mouth lowered to hers.

After four days of resistance, she couldn't seem to muster the strength to even whisper a *no*. She could only melt under his touch, catch fire with the first stroke of his tongue along her lips. Ease back against the sofa at his urging.

Shani had no idea how far things would have gone if the phone hadn't rung. The first trill didn't register, the second brought Logan's head up, frustration in his face. The third brought him to his feet, leaving Shani to clear her mind and come to her senses.

As he barked out a hello to whoever had phoned, Shani quickly gathered her notebook and textbooks. Keeping her head down, she waved at him as she headed for the door.

"Hold on," he spat out as he dropped the phone and hurried through the living room after her. "Shani!"

She kept on going, slipping outside. He shouted her name again as she reached the bottom of the stairs. Without looking back, she ran toward the cottage, closing her ears to his third imperious summons.

If Logan had known the caller was his father, he would have let the phone ring, despite the fortuitous interruption of his folly with Shani. Once he saw the number on his caller ID, he nearly let it go to voice mail, particularly when Shani all but ran from his house. But his father only called when he wanted something and wouldn't give up until he got it. Shani wouldn't be coming back tonight. Logan might as well deal with whatever unpleasantness his father had called about.

When it was clear that Shani wouldn't return, he grabbed up the phone again. "Hello, Dad."

"How are you, son? It's been a long time."

A month since Logan had last called. He'd phoned on his father's birthday, then every day for nearly a week afterward. Colin Rafferty had never answered, hadn't bothered to return Logan's call. He hadn't acknowledged the gift certificate Logan had sent, either.

Not that it mattered to Logan. He'd long ago given up caring.

Just tell me what you want so we can get this over with. He longed to say the words out loud, but instead, he asked, "What's up, Dad?"

"Still having trouble recovering from that last setback," Colin said. "Cash flow's not looking too good."

That "last setback" had been tax evasion. Colin Rafferty had driven Logan's grandfather's once-profitable import/export business into the ground in record time with shady deals and well-cooked books. The company that Colin Rafferty Sr. had built into a powerhouse, Colin Jr. had destroyed with twenty years of fraud. Only the family name and copious amounts from Logan's trust fund had kept his father out of prison.

But the high life was over, the mansion and Jaguar gone, the lavish parties a thing of the past. Logan supported his father with an allowance, but Colin Rafferty never did understand how to stick to a budget.

"I'll talk to the accountant," Logan told him. "How much do you need?"

When his father named the amount, Logan nearly exploded. He had just managed to reel in his temper when his father said, "I heard a rumor from your sister-in-law."

Logan bit back an oath. His father had always found Arianna's generous sister Corinna a soft touch. Apparently he was still hitting her up for money. Logan wouldn't have thought Corinna would have let the secret out, but he knew how persuasive Colin could be.

"Leave Arianna's family alone. They're not your private piggy bank."

"Just called to say hello," Colin insisted. "But those babies—what in God's name are you going to do with them?"

"Baby," Logan clarified, although he wasn't sure why he bothered. "There's only one."

"Kids are a pain in the butt," Colin said. "I ought to know."

Logan might have believed his father if he'd actually had anything to do with Logan's upbringing. But over the years, Logan had seen more of his various nannies than he ever had his father.

But wouldn't he be doing the same with his own child? He'd have to hire someone to look after the baby. The kind of hours he worked, he might see them just as little as his own father had seen him.

No. It would be different. He'd make sure of it.

"I've got to go, Dad. I'll have the accountant transfer the money." His thumb drifted to the disconnect button.

But his father wasn't finished. "You don't really think you're going be all warm and cuddly with this kid of yours, do you? You damn well ought to know by now that old fatherly-love thing just isn't in the Rafferty genes."

For an instant Logan flashed back to the day his mother had died, a scared, grieving little boy left with the cold piece of work that was his father. Acid burned in the pit of his stomach as he squelched the memory.

"Thanks for the feedback," Logan said, then hung up the phone and dropped it on the kitchen counter.

The days of him trying desperately to please his father, to earn his praise, were long gone. But somehow dear old Dad still had the weapons to jab and pierce. Despite the fact that his father was a failure times three—as a husband, as a father, as a businessman—a part of Logan still reacted to Colin Rafferty's gibes.

Without conscious thought, Logan found himself moving toward the door, exiting the house to stand out on the front porch. Light spilled from the cottage windows, the warm glow drawing him down the stairs to the decomposed granite walkway. He forced himself to stop there when what he really wanted to do was to stride across those dozen or so yards and pound on Shani's door.

She needed her rest. He needed to keep his hands off her.

Knowing that didn't change the urgency burning in him to pull her into his arms, to hold her, to contemplate the life burgeoning inside her. Breathing her scent, feeling her skin against his, maybe he'd be able to banish the doubts that haunted him. Maybe he'd find a way to remake the sorry legacy his father had bequeathed him.

And maybe the world would spin the other way on its axis. Because not even Shani could perform that miracle.

Chapter Eight

Determined to both avoid Logan and to maximize her time working on her extra-credit project, Shani holed herself up in the cottage all of Saturday morning and early afternoon. She even toiled through lunch, munching a hastily slapped-together sandwich while she typed at her laptop. When she came up for air, first draft completed, she was surprised to discover it was only three o'clock.

Leaving the laptop on the kitchen table, she rose to stretch her legs and considered what to do next. She could start her rewrite, keeping her nose to the grindstone right up until seven o'clock when Logan would come by to pick her up. But she'd prefer setting the work aside until tomorrow morning, attacking it again with a fresh eye.

Wandering over to the front window, she angled herself so she could see the main house. Logan had gone out this morning, but had since returned—his Mercedes was back in the drive. Temptation whispered in her ear, suggesting she should go over to the house. Just to say hello, to let him know how well she'd done today.

Except she was kidding herself if a hello and a discussion of her project was what she really wanted. Her body was clamoring to stoke the heat she and Logan had sparked last night, not to engage in intellectual discourse on industrial organization.

She needed to get out of the cottage. The five minutes she'd spent this morning digging through her closet for something suitable for tonight had left her in despair. The one formal gown that might have sufficed would no longer zip past her waist. She felt even more hopeless after a peek at the Web site for the fund-raising gala. Photos from previous years showed women wearing lavish, knockout gowns to the event. Dresses that were far beyond anything Shani owned.

Picking up the phone, Shani called her friend Julie Mendoza, and arranged to meet her at the Roseville Galleria. The shopping gene most women seemed to possess had skipped a generation in Shani. Julie, six years younger and more in touch with what was fashionable, was delighted at the prospect of finding Shani a dress for the gala.

Julie had been a rock for Shani after Arianna's death last year. The life Julie had led had been as carefree as Shani's had been difficult, but the young girl had a bottomless well of empathy for other people's troubles. When Arianna's death had triggered a self-examination in Shani, had her thinking that perhaps she ought to give up her dream of a college degree and go back home to Iowa, it was Julie who had encouraged her to stick to her goal.

Since then, Julie had been a sounding board whenever

Shani needed to vent. So far, she was the only one besides her mother and sister who knew about the surrogacy.

An hour and a half into their shopping expedition, after visiting nearly every dress store in the expansive Galleria, they were still empty-handed. Everything on the racks either had Julie wrinkling her nose in disapproval or sent Shani and her bank balance into sticker shock.

"No," she told Julie firmly as the blonde pulled out yet another outrageously expensive dress. "Have you seen the price tag?"

"Come on, you only live once," Julie cajoled. Easy for Julie to say. She still lived at home and her parents were footing the bill for the master's degree in nursing she'd just started.

"It won't fit, anyway," Shani told her. "Size six. I'm an eight."

"You were a six last summer when I lent you my dress." Julie gave Shani's body a quick once-over. "Have you put on that much weight?"

"Enough." Shani rested her hand on her tummy. "Mostly in my waist."

Julie cast an appraising eye along Shani's body. "What are you, about eight weeks now?"

"Nearly nine."

When Shani had confided in Julie about her agreement to act as a gestational carrier, she'd glossed over some of the details. Out of deference to Logan's privacy, Shani kept Logan's name out of the explanation, leading Julie to believe the genetic parents were strangers to her.

"Maybe Daddy ought to pay for the dress," Julie said. "He's responsible for the change in your figure."

Shani laughed. "I don't think a clothing allowance is part of the deal."

"Hey, you're living at his house," Julie said.

"In a guest cottage."

"On his estate," Julie persisted. "Who is this guy? You never told me."

Shani just shook her head. "I haven't got much more time to spare. We have to either find a dress or head back."

Realization lit Julie's face. "You're not going to the gala with this guy? With the father?"

Shani checked her watch. "I have twenty minutes. Are we still shopping, or do I go home?"

But Julie wasn't giving up. "You're crossing over a line here, Shani. If you're a GC for the father, I don't know that a personal relationship is all that great an idea."

"It's not a personal relationship," Shani told her, heat rising in her cheeks.

"If you're going out with him, it is."

"I know him," Shani finally confessed. "From before. He was Arianna's husband."

Julie's eyes widened. "The jerk? The complete horse's— What were you thinking, Shani?"

"It's a long story and I'm not up to telling it. I need to get going." She groped in her purse for her car keys.

"But you hate that guy! How could you have agreed to be his surrogate?"

Shani turned her back on Julie, head bent to her purse to avoid her friend's gaze. "It's complicated."

"Wait." Julie turned Shani toward her, her sharp gaze studying Shani's face. "You're not falling for this guy, are you?"

No! Of course not. Shani shouted the words in her head, but somehow they got stuck in her throat. "Why in the world would you say such a crazy thing?" she asked instead.

Julie's expression turned serious. "That would be beyond bad, Shani."

"Of course it would," Shani agreed, exiting the store. "I do have to get going."

Keeping pace with her, Julie took Shani's arm. "There's one more shop we can try. The owner is a friend of my mom's."

The dress Julie unearthed from the sale rack at Sassy's was like nothing Shani had ever worn, an ankle-length raspberry silk confection she likely never would have tried on. But the backless halter-top gown with its loose waist fit perfectly, and the price, after the shop owner added a discount, didn't make nearly the dent in Shani's checking account that she'd expected.

It was past six by the time Shani made it back to the cottage. Barely enough time to shower and do something with her hair. It was too short to put up—maybe she could scoop it back with a pair of combs. She'd add glittery earrings and Arianna's necklace, then keep warm with a hip-length black velvet cape she'd found in a thrift store a few years ago.

As Shani hurried to get ready, Julie's preposterous question echoed in her mind. *You're not falling for this guy, are you?* What could Julie have seen in Shani's face to make her ask that? Admittedly, Shani found herself preoccupied with Logan, thoughts of him stealing into her mind most hours of the day and night. But she was carrying his baby, living on his estate, working at his company. It only made sense that she would think of him.

It had nothing to do with how she felt about him. She felt the same as always toward Logan…didn't she? She wasn't as angry as she'd been back in the days when Arianna had so often cried on her shoulder. And she didn't dislike him as she once had. But she felt nothing for Logan beyond a certain mutual respect.

Assured that Julie's question had simply been out of

left field, Shani fastened her cape around her shoulders
and grabbed a small black clutch bag. Logan knocked
just as she switched off the bedroom light, and she
hurried to answer the door.

When Logan had wrapped up a slice of Mrs. Singh's
pecan pie to take over to the cottage this afternoon, he'd
been looking forward to a few moments spent with
Shani. He'd thought maybe he could look over what
she'd written so far, give her feedback, clarify any points
she was still having difficulty with.

But as he stepped out on the porch, he realized her
car wasn't there. He'd let himself into the cottage,
guilt twinging because he knew she wouldn't like it,
on the pretext of leaving the pie for her in the refrigerator. But while inside, he looked for some indica-
tion of where she might have gone. He saw only the
closed laptop on the kitchen table with a neat stack of
paper beside it.

He returned to the house agitated and restless. At a
loss for what to do until Shani returned, he pulled out
the large mixing bowl Mrs. Singh had shoved in the
back of a cupboard. Bread-making had been his therapy
from his early teens, when he'd been an angry, resent-
ful kid on the edge of getting into serious trouble. One
of the housekeepers had taught him the basics one day.

He did it all by hand, from the first mixing of flour and
yeast to kneading the sticky dough into a soft warm ball.
But not even the perfume of freshly baked bread had
eased his restiveness as he waited for Shani to come back
home. It had been all he could do to keep from storming
over there when she pulled in just after six. He'd forced
himself to wait until seven, taking time dressing for a
fund-raising event he had no desire to attend.

Now, standing on Shani's doorstep, Logan strafed her with his gaze, from the sleek dark brown hair held back with combs, past the black velvet cape, to her toes peeking from the hem of her dress. As he stared, she slipped past him, shivering in the chilly November air. The faintest drift of her perfume lingered in her wake.

With her beside him in the car, her fragrance tantalized him, confused him as they started down the driveway. "You left today." He said it clumsily, wincing at the accusation in his tone.

She gave him a hard look. "So did you."

"I had to pick up some papers at the office. I thought you were spending the day working."

"I did." She narrowed her gaze on him. "Are you checking up on me?"

The driver's-side window had fogged over, so he lowered it to check traffic to the left before making his turn from the private road onto the main thoroughfare. The brisk air mingled with her scent, but did nothing to clear his befuddled mind.

Rolling the window up again, he forced a more even tone to his words. "You were concerned you wouldn't have enough time to finish your project."

"You're a good teacher. I was able to finish the first draft." Something in the side-view mirror caught her eye and she twisted to look through the Mercedes' back window. After a moment, she straightened again. "I had time to do some shopping."

"Alone?" He felt ridiculous asking the question, but he couldn't seem to stop himself.

"With a friend." He heard her huff of impatience. "A female friend, for heaven's sake."

Now he felt even more like a fool. Pulling onto the

freeway, he flexed his hands to relax them. "Did you want me to look over your draft?"

"I'd appreciate that." Another glance over her shoulder, then she settled back. "Have you thought about how you'll introduce me tonight?"

He'd been so preoccupied with getting her to agree to come with him, it had never crossed his mind. "You're one of my employees."

"You're dating one of your employees?"

"No." He raked his fingers through his hair, struggling to get his brain in gear. "Who would ask that?"

"They might not say it out loud, but they'll wonder."

"Then we tell them what?" he asked, exasperation tightening the tension in him.

She thought a moment. "I'm an old friend of Arianna's. When you had an opening at your table, you gave me a call."

It seemed a reasonable explanation. If he didn't look at Shani all night, managed to keep his hands off her. Even the most clueless attendee at the gala would know there was something more between him and Shani if he didn't keep his inconvenient libido under control.

Which he realized would be a near-impossible task once they'd entered the conference center and he helped her off with her cape. His jaw literally dropped at his first glimpse of the back of Shani's breathtaking dress. Baring the nape of her neck to the base of her spine, the silky raspberry-colored gown couldn't have draped more perfectly on her beautiful body.

Fighting against the impulse to stroke the long sweep of golden skin, he stood rooted on the spot, blind to others crowding around him at the coat check. It wasn't until Shani turned toward him, smiling up at him, presenting him with the more demure front of the dark pink gown, that he was able to kick-start his brain again.

"Where are we sitting?" she asked, apparently oblivious to his raging hormones.

"I reserved a table near the front." He gestured toward the door of the ballroom.

As she moved toward the entry, she took an awkward step. He took her arm to steady her, one hand on her bare shoulder. The softness of her skin took his breath away.

"Not used to heels, I'm afraid," she said as her fingers wrapped around the sleeve of his suit.

He tucked her arm firmly in the crook of his. "Your body's changing, too."

She flicked him a surprised glance. "Has it?"

He felt heat rush to his face. He'd noticed every altered curve of her fuller cheeks, the softening of the line of her jaw. All the time he'd spent with her lately, at dinners and during their study sessions, he'd memorized her every feature.

Not that he'd tell her that. "I know Arianna's did. She only put on a few pounds at the beginning, but that small difference affected her balance."

"I suppose you're right. The first time…" Her voice faded out for a moment. "I think I had too much else on my mind to notice."

As they wound through the tables filling the massive ballroom, more than one curious gaze turned their way. Logan recognized several people and acknowledged their attention with a nod. If they wondered who Shani was, they were too polite to come over and grill him about her. Most of them wealthy and very private people themselves, they would likely allow Logan the courtesy of keeping his secrets to himself.

There were a few photographers, however, one of

them from the charity that had organized the event, but the others were from the press. With any luck, if they photographed Logan and Shani, they'd ask for names only and wouldn't pry into their relationship.

Logan found the placards with his and Shani's name and pulled out her chair. Four of the other six had already seated themselves, clients of Good Sport that he'd invited to join him, plus their spouses.

He introduced Shani around the table, mentioning her connection to Arianna and her position as an intern at MiniSport. No one so much as blinked an eye as she greeted the others in their group.

"Jack is running late," Bill Fredericks, owner of a chain of soccer-equipment stores, told Logan. "He and his wife had some appointment after work."

They shouted small talk across the table, the clamor of several hundred people packed into the cavernous space making it difficult to hear. With an effort, Logan kept his eyes forward, across the circle at Bill's middle-aged wife, while his attention drifted again and again to Shani's bare shoulder just inches from his.

He was grateful for the arrival of Jack Helms, Good Sport's first and now largest customer. In the years since Jack's chain of specialty water-sports stores bought their initial shipment of graphite kayak paddles from Logan's company, they'd developed a friendship of sorts. Jack and his wife, Patricia, had occasionally joined Arianna and Logan for dinner or a local theater production.

Logan got to his feet as Patricia approached, but before he could introduce Shani to Jack's wife, the woman smiled with apparent delight and leaned over to give Shani a hug before sitting beside her. "I didn't know you would be here."

"It's good to see you, too," Shani said. "How's Junior?"

"You know each other?" Logan asked as he seated himself again.

"We met at the clinic," Shani said.

"And I dragged her out to lunch one day when I needed some moral support."

Now Logan saw Patricia's rounded belly and realized the woman was several months pregnant. If his mind hadn't been so hazed by the scent and texture of Shani's skin, he might have remembered Jack confiding that he and Patricia were having some of the same struggles to start a family that Logan and Arianna had had. Jack had taken his wife's two miscarriages hard.

Shani leaned close enough to murmur into Logan's ear. "She only knows I'm acting as a surrogate, not who the father is."

But Jack had a speculative look on his face, and Logan realized his friend was putting two and two together. No doubt Patricia had mentioned Shani to Jack and he'd made the connection seeing Shani with Logan.

Jack wasn't the type to press Logan for personal information, but the question was clear in Jack's face. Because of their history, Logan felt an obligation to say something. Shani's pregnancy would become common knowledge soon enough. Maybe telling Jack would break the ice.

The start of dinner offered a reprieve. An army of waiters served salads and bread, followed by overseasoned chicken marsala and gummy rice. One speaker after another stepped up to the podium as everyone ate, inspirational speeches from previous recipients of the charity's largesse interspersed with thanks for the donors' generosity. An inexplicable anxiety built in Logan as he made his way through the rubber chicken and stale rolls. He wanted nothing more than to center his hand on Shani's back, to feel her warmth, to take comfort in the contact. He took one bite of the cloyingly sweet chocolate mousse, then pushed it back and dropped his napkin on the table.

Pushing his chair back, he rose, lightly resting his fingers on Shani's shoulder. She tore herself from her conversation with Patricia and smiled up at him. It took everything in him not to pull her to her feet and into his arms.

"I need some air."

As he stepped away, he glanced back over his shoulder at Jack. As expected, his friend rose as well. "I'll join you."

They traced a serpentine route through the packed ballroom toward the exits. Once outside, by silent mutual agreement, they moved off past the smokers clustered near the doors. Walking slowly, they made their way down K Street, the pedestrian thoroughfare bisected by light rail tracks.

Jack spoke first. "I take it the baby is yours and Arianna's."

"Yes."

"How far along?"

They paused under a street lamp and the chill seeped in past Logan's suit coat. "We're past the eight-week mark. Only one baby, but everything is going well."

Jack nodded and stared off down the dark street. "I confess I'm surprised."

Logan's earlier anxiety kicked up again. "Why?"

"At the time, you made it pretty clear the baby thing was Arianna's idea. I would have thought you'd be glad not to have the obligation anymore."

Jack's words echoed what Logan's father had said. The reminder heightened Logan's uneasiness. He could ignore his feckless father's ramblings, but to hear it from a friend gave the words greater weight.

"I wasn't aware I gave that impression," Logan said.

"One night we talked about the responsibility of having children," Jack said, his breath fogging in the cold air. "When we were at that convention back east. I was worried about how much traveling I was doing, if I'd be able to be home enough to raise my kids. You just shrugged and said, I'm leaving that to Arianna."

Logan cringed. He remembered that night, how exhausted he'd been after the day, glad-handing dozens of would-be customers. He and Jack had been dawdling in the bar and all Logan could think about was crawling into bed. At the time, he couldn't fathom having the energy to read a bedtime story or tucking in his son or daughter. It had been a relief to recall that that would be Arianna's job.

But it was different now, wasn't it? Because Arianna wasn't here, because the baby had no one but him. By default, he'd have to be a better father than he would have been when Arianna was alive.

Doubt dug a hollow in the pit of his stomach. Logan ruthlessly smothered his misgivings.

"Let's just say I've had a change of heart," he told Jack.

He could see the troubled look in Jack's eyes. "That's good. I'm glad to hear it."

They headed back inside. The November chill biting Logan's skin was nothing compared to the chunk of ice that froze his insides. He put on a good face as he rejoined the table, laughing at a slightly off-color joke Bill told, making a show of attentiveness when the woman to his right pulled out photos of her grandkids. He wanted desperately to go home, to be alone with Shani, to absorb her peace.

An interminable hour later, they headed back to the

parking garage and climbed into the Mercedes. Before
he started the car, he shut his eyes, leaning back against
the headrest, willing the tension to leave him.

"What is it?" Shani asked, her soft voice the balm he
needed.

His conversation with Jack turned over in his mind,
an endless loop replaying. His father's harsh assess-
ment of Logan's lack of paternal instinct blared in dis-
sonant counterpoint.

Opening his eyes, he turned to Shani. The sweet
empathy in her face pulled the question from him.

"What if I don't love the baby? Can I still be a
good father?"

Shock rippled across her face, a moment only before
she suppressed it. He could see her struggle to formu-
late an answer.

"Never mind," he rasped out as he twisted the
ignition key.

"Logan—"

"Never mind!"

Backing from the parking space, he navigated the
turns of the garage a little too fast, tires screeching. He
refused to look at Shani, didn't want to see the pity, or
worse, in her eyes.

It was just as well, or he might have hit the dark
green Nissan that roared around him and cut him off
on L Street. As it was, he had to slam on the brakes to
avoid hitting the car before it made a hard right up
Tenth Street.

Shani's gasp pulled his attention toward her. She'd
gone pale with fear.

"We didn't hit him." Logan resisted the urge to reach
for her hand.

She glanced at him, taking a breath as if to speak.

Then she looked away with a little shake of her head. "It just startled me."

He had the uneasy sense there was more to it than that. Maybe their conversation earlier had stirred misgivings in her about his ability to care for the baby.

If that was the case, he'd just as soon not know.

Chapter Nine

Four days later, Shani was crammed up against the window of the small regional jet carrying her and Logan from their layover in Chicago to Eastern Iowa Airport. Beside her, Logan pored over a stack of department-status reports, his knees skimming the seat in front of him, his shoulders brushing hers. Shani gazed out the window, watching for her first view of Cedar Rapids.

When Shani had first talked to her mother about the trip home for Thanksgiving, her plans had not included Logan. But then Barbara Jacoby asked what Logan would be doing for the holiday. Shani had already asked Logan the question and had received the unsurprising answer that he planned to work around the house. When Shani relayed that information to her mother, Mrs. Jacoby did an end run around Shani, calling Logan directly to invite him for the weekend.

According to Logan, Shani's mother refused to allow

him to decline. So here he was beside her, marching into yet another part of Shani's life.

She couldn't muster much annoyance at her mother's invitation. Her heart had ached at the thought of Logan spending the weekend alone. Thanksgiving had always been a time for all of her family to gather; she couldn't imagine eating a solitary dinner that day.

The plane shuddered slightly as it made its descent into Iowa. She spotted the brown swaths of fallow cornfields as they drew closer to the airport, and nostalgia tugged at her. Although there were seasonal changes in the Sacramento area, she missed the ebb and flow of crops and weather from her childhood in Iowa City.

Logan stuffed away his paperwork, then straightened, leaning toward her slightly as he tightened his seat belt. "I could have bowed out at the last minute. Told your mother something came up."

"It's fine, Logan," Shani assured him, just as she had yesterday when he'd brought it up then. "My mother will love having someone new to fuss over."

"And she understands our arrangement. She doesn't think you and I…"

"She knows," Shani told him emphatically.

Except Shani wasn't sure if *she* knew anymore. Ever since that day she and Julie went shopping, Shani's emotions had been in an even greater tumult than before. Logan seemed to permeate every corner of her existence, as much a part of her as her own skin, the breath she drew and exhaled.

It had to be the baby growing inside her. As long as she was pregnant with Logan's child, she wouldn't be able to completely separate herself from him.

They exited the plane, Shani's carry-on bag slung over Logan's shoulder. He hadn't let her tote any of her own luggage, glaring at her when she so much as laid a finger on the larger rolling suitcase before they'd checked it in Sacramento. He probably would have insisted she ride on the luggage cart if he'd thought he could persuade her.

Logan handled the retrieval of their suitcases and the rental of a Lincoln Town Car with the ease of someone well accustomed to traveling. They were on their way to her family's ranch-style home in southwest Iowa City in much less time than it would have taken Shani on her own.

Dusk had fallen by the time they'd pulled into the driveway, the lengthening shadows of late afternoon overcome by approaching darkness. The lights glowing in the windows of the white frame house set off a spurt of joy inside Shani as she imagined her mother and sister waiting for her inside.

"There's nothing like coming home," Shani said softly.

Her gaze sweeping across the front of the house, she glanced over at Logan. The expression on his face squeezed her heart even tighter. The Logan she knew—arrogant, imperious, take-charge—had for the moment faded away. In place of the man was the boy, the yearning, the longing clear in his face.

"What was home like for you?" she asked, although she suspected she knew.

"No home. Not like this, anyway." He pushed open his door, forestalling any further discussion.

Rachael answered the front door, squealing with delight and grabbing Shani into a Heimlich-strength hug. "You don't look the least bit pregnant."

"Almost twelve weeks," Shani told her.

Her gaze roved over the familiar cozy living room. A fire burned in the woodstove, its heat permeating the

If offer card is missing write to: Silhouette Reader Service, 3010 Walden Ave., P.O. Box 1867, Buffalo NY 14240-1867

NO POSTAGE
NECESSARY
IF MAILED
IN THE
UNITED STATES

BUSINESS REPLY MAIL
FIRST-CLASS MAIL   PERMIT NO. 717   BUFFALO, NY

POSTAGE WILL BE PAID BY ADDRESSEE

SILHOUETTE READER SERVICE
3010 WALDEN AVE
PO BOX 1867
BUFFALO NY 14240-9952

Do You Have the LUCKY KEY?

PLAY THE Lucky Key Game

and you can get

FREE BOOKS and FREE GIFTS!

Scratch the gold areas with a coin. Then check below to see the books and gifts you can get!

YES!

I have scratched off the gold areas. Please send me the 2 FREE BOOKS and 2 FREE GIFTS, worth about $10, for which I qualify. I understand I am under no obligation to purchase any books, as explained on the back of this card.

335 SDL ERT7   **235 SDL ERXV**

FIRST NAME	LAST NAME

ADDRESS

APT.#	CITY

STATE/PROV.   ZIP/POSTAL CODE

www.eHarlequin.com

🔑🔑🔑🔑 2 free books plus 2 free gifts   🔑🔑🔑🔑 1 free book

🔑🔑🔑🔑 2 free books   🔑🔑🔑🔑 Try Again!

DETACH AND MAIL CARD TODAY!

(S-SE-03/08)

© 2007 HARLEQUIN ENTERPRISES LIMITED ® and ™ are trademarks owned and used by the trademark owner and/or its licensee.

comfortable space. Shani had grown up in this room—
watching television sprawled on that same worn
recliner, doing her homework at the antique desk in the
corner, daydreaming in the bay window. Her mother had
replaced the sofa in the past few years, but much of the
other furniture Shani remembered from childhood. She
wondered if she would still be able to read hers and
Rachael's initials on the underside of the coffee table.

Her mother's embrace was more gentle than
Rachael's, then Shani was passed along to Aunt Helen,
Uncle Dave and their two young boys. She introduced
Logan around. He offered handshakes to everyone, in-
cluding her six- and eight-year-old cousins, Aaron and
Ben. Her mother ignored his hand and gave him the
same affectionate hug she'd given Shani.

Logan looked startled, but he smiled as he drew away
from Shani's mother. "I see where Shani gets her beauty,
Mrs. Jacoby," he said.

The compliment completely caught Shani's mother
off guard. She laughed and fluttered her hands at Logan.
"Call me Barbara. Dave, help Logan with the suitcases.
I'll go get supper on the table."

They gathered in the dining room, where her mother
had set out the good china for the adults and the
everyday for the two boys. They passed around brisket,
roast potatoes and a green salad the boys refused to eat
until they saw Logan pile it high on his plate.

Logan held his own in the clamor of conversation
around the table, he and Uncle Dave comparing notes
on the differences in the business climate in California
and Iowa. Shani was pleasantly surprised with how he
interacted with her two awestruck cousins, asking them
about school, whether or not they liked sports. When he
promised them each a soccer ball, set of cleats and a

carry bag with a Hawkeyes logo, their jaws dropped in admiration.

Again and again, his gaze drifted across the table to Shani, as if he was assuring himself she was still there. Each brief glance set off a glow within her, filled her with a gladness that she'd brought him home with her.

At one point, Logan smiled at something one of her mischievous cousins said, then lifted his gaze to Shani. She smiled back, a spark of connection shooting between them. Only an instant, then she tore her gaze away.

And caught her mother watching her. Mrs. Jacoby raised one brow in query. Shani shook her head and focused back on her brisket. She didn't want to know what her mother might have made of Shani's incautious smile.

After dinner, as Shani's mother served up apple cobbler à la mode, she told Logan, "I've made up Shani's old room for you."

"That's not necessary," he said as he took a dish of warm dessert from Ben. "I have a reservation at a motel in Coralville."

"Shani will be sleeping in Rachael's room," Mrs. Jacoby said. "Why stay at a motel when I have the space?"

Logan looked over at Shani. "I appreciate the hospitality."

After they'd finished the cobbler and her aunt and uncle left with their two sleepy boys, Shani took Logan aside in the living room. "You don't have to stay."

"I don't mind." He held his hands out to the fire's warmth.

"I could tell her you need the quiet to do some work."

He turned to her. "You don't want me here?"

"I'm glad you're here." As soon as she said the words out loud, she realized he might misinterpret them. "I mean, I'm glad you're not spending the holiday alone. I just wasn't sure if you'd be comfortable."

He stared down at the orange flames glowing through the glass of the woodstove. "I don't know if I've ever been as comfortable as I've been tonight."

Logan soon learned that the gregarious dinner on the eve of Thanksgiving was just a warm-up for the main event. Family started arriving at eleven—aunts, uncles, cousins. Shani's paternal grandmother, Ida—apparently still involved with the extended family even though her absent son no longer was—showed up in the early afternoon. They installed the old woman by the fire, her walker at hand, where she commandeered the youngest children, including a baby girl.

Although he'd always had a talent for remembering names, Logan gave up the effort to remember who was who after the introduction of what must have been the twentieth second cousin. It didn't seem to matter with the Jacobys and Beckensteins. They pulled him into their conversations, anyway, into their impromptu football games on the front lawn, their cutthroat games of Oh, Hell. Deprived nearly all his life of family, Logan felt as if he'd been tossed into an ocean of loving affection.

When it was finally time to sit down to the meal, whose aroma had been tantalizing them all day, they had to rearrange the living room and split into three groups— kids in the kitchen, ten around the dining room table and the rest around rented tables in the living room. Logan sat opposite Grandma Ida's spot by the fire, with Shani directly to his right. He'd only gotten glimpses of her during the day as she helped her mother in the kitchen. He was grateful to have a few moments with her.

She leaned close to be heard over the noise of a dozen voices. "Ready to run screaming into the night?"

He should have been. Families like Shani's were entirely out of his experience. Even Arianna had only a few living relatives who were involved in her life.

"They're good people," Logan said.

The corners of her mouth turned up. "Uncle Wallace hasn't brought out his accordion yet."

He couldn't help himself—he laughed, the sound carrying to the far end of the table where Shani's Uncle Dave sat with his wife. "You shouldn't be telling Logan those naughty jokes, Grandma Ida."

Laughter rippled around the table at that, and Logan felt himself even more tightly bound up with this family, with Shani. But he wasn't truly a part of this warm, raucous group. Despite their acceptance, his presence in their lives was temporary. Once Shani gave birth to his child, they'd be gone just as she would be.

He ignored the ache that centered in his chest at the thought. He'd find a way to create a family for his son or daughter. Although he'd lost touch with Arianna's sister, Corinna, and their parents when Arianna died, Corinna had seemed happy when he told her about the baby. They all lived back east, so they wouldn't likely see the child much, but at least there'd be some family.

Yet another issue he hadn't fully thought through. He felt overwhelmed by failure before his child was even born.

Without conscious thought, he reached for Shani's hand, folding his fingers around hers under the table. She looked up at him, brow furrowed slightly, lips parting as if to ask why he'd made contact. He couldn't answer, couldn't have put into words why he needed her so desperately in that moment.

Shani must have seen something in his face because she squeezed his hand and asked, "What?"

He shook his head slowly and returned his hand to his own lap where it belonged. He had no answer for her, didn't understand himself the maelstrom inside him. As he grappled with the unfamiliar emotions, his attention strayed down the table to where Barbara Jacoby sat.

She stared at him, her expression thoughtful, troubled. She couldn't have seen him take Shani's hand under the table, couldn't have read the thoughts in his mind. But somehow, she knew.

After the meal came cleanup, a community project involving a conga line of kids carrying dinner plates, bowls and platters, and a group of young adults taking charge of packaging leftovers for family members to take home with them. The kids cleared and the men washed the dishes, Dave at the sink, Logan and Wallace drying and stacking. Shani helped her mother put the finishing touches on dessert, her radiant face filling Logan with an unfamiliar contentment.

After chocolate pecan pie and pumpkin cake, they gathered around the cleared tables for hands of hearts and Russian rummy. Shani organized the kids around the coffee table for Go Fish and Old Maid and quickly had them in stitches. She was irresistible, not only for the youngsters, but for Logan. He bowed out of the adults' card games to join her, stretching his long legs clear to the other side of the table, where Shani's nine-month-old cousin sprawled on his ankles.

Eventually everyone filtered out, the parents of the youngest first, as their charges grew tired and cranky. Then the oldsters, Ida, Uncle Wallace and Great-Aunt

Maude. Dave and Helen were the last to leave after helping Logan fold up the rented tables.

All during the evening, Logan could sense Shani's mother's focus on him. Unless he planned to hide in the guest room until he and Shani left on Saturday, he couldn't avoid the private talk she obviously wanted.

So when Shani went to Rachael's room to get ready for bed, Logan hung back, picking up a few last glasses and dessert plates that had been left behind in the living room. He found Mrs. Jacoby in the kitchen, nursing a cup of coffee.

"Would you like some?" she asked. "I think there's one more cup in the pot."

"Sure," he said, although he'd had his fill.

She poured the dark brew into a mug, then passed him the creamer and a spoon. She'd remembered how he liked his coffee, her attentiveness reminding him of Shani.

She gazed at him over her cup. "You're not at all what I expected."

He took a sip. "Is that good or bad?"

"Shani hasn't mentioned you often over the years." Her direct gaze didn't leave his face. "But when she did, she was never flattering."

He laughed softly. "I'm not surprised."

"I didn't think you'd be an ogre. I just thought you'd be sitting in a corner somewhere, pounding on a computer keyboard."

"Did you know my wife?" he asked.

She shook her head. "Shani invited her out here more than once. She never accepted the invitation."

Mrs. Jacoby leaned a hip against the tile counter as she eyed him. Slender as her daughter, she was shorter, more diminutive. Even still, under her scrutiny, Logan felt a bit like a small boy called on the carpet.

She delivered the volley he'd been expecting. "What's going on between you and Shani?"

"She's gestational carrier for my baby. Nothing beyond that."

"That's a load of hooey. I've seen the way you two look at each other." Her gaze narrowed. "Are you and she—"

"No!" He felt his face heat. It crossed his mind to tell her it was none of her business, but he knew that gambit wouldn't fly with the protective Mrs. Jacoby. "We're not in any kind of relationship."

"Except you are," she said softly. "She's nurturing your baby inside her, giving you a gift beyond price. There will always be a relationship between the two of you."

She'd spelled out what he hadn't wanted to acknowledge—that no matter how hard he tried to make his interaction with Shani businesslike and professional, the reality was different. They were connected in the most intimate way, even if he never touched Shani again, never kissed her. He and she would always be a part of each other.

The realization staggered him, so much so that he was completely unprepared for Mrs. Jacoby's bombshell. "It's going to kill her to give up this child."

"She's known from the start—"

"It doesn't matter," she said. "Her head might have persuaded her she could handle this, but it will break her heart."

Even as he sensed the truth of what she said, Logan felt helpless to change the inevitable. "She agreed" was all he could think to say.

She nodded. "There is one way to change things. Except I'm not so sure it would be right."

"It wouldn't," he told her, guessing what she was suggesting.

"Maybe not," she acknowledged. "But I can see you do feel something for her already."

But he didn't. Even if he did, Shani didn't feel anything for him. "We're just friends." And barely even that.

"Still, what would it hurt, Logan?" Mrs. Jacoby said quietly, thoughtfully. "What would it hurt if you married her?"

Rachael was already asleep by the time Shani returned from her shower, warm and cozy in flannel pajamas. Her sister had left a small light burning on the bedside table, so Shani could curl up in bed and read a bit before she went to sleep. After the activity of the day, and her constant awareness of Logan's nearness, she needed to find a way to unwind.

But she'd finished the book she'd brought on the plane and hadn't remembered to bring another. No doubt her mother would have a book or magazine Shani could borrow.

As she started down the hall to her mother's room, she heard voices from the kitchen. She peered far enough around the corner to spot Logan and her mother. Ducking back in the hallway so they wouldn't see her, Shani wondered what kind of motherly talk Logan had been roped into.

She considered just returning to Rachael's room and turning out the light, but curiosity over Logan's and her mother's discussion only ratcheted up Shani's tension. Moving quickly past the open doorway, she hurried to her old room at the other end of the hall. She'd left behind a stack of well-loved novels in the corner of her closet. She'd go grab an old favorite and be out of there again before Logan showed up.

Her mother had moved her sewing machine into

Shani's old bedroom and had replaced Shani's large dresser with a smaller one tucked into the corner. The feminine bed with its white wrought-iron bedstead and frilly comforter hadn't changed, though. Seeing the lacy spread brought back a rush of memories of her teenage years, when Shani lay on that bed and dreamed of what her life might be.

It took her a few moments to find the books—her mother had packed them in a box and slid them under the bed. Sitting cross-legged on the floor, she'd just made a selection from the box and was about to return the books under the bed when Logan entered the room.

She tried to get her feet under her, to rise quickly from the floor, but her changing body thwarted her. She banged an elbow on the nightstand, swayed and might have fallen over if Logan hadn't covered the distance between them in two long strides.

He caught her by the elbows, holding her until she was steady. Her heart hammered in her ears as he towered over her, his expression serious, heat rolling off him in waves. She took a breath, heard it rasping in her ears.

She had to think of something besides the touch of his hands, the way his mouth would feel on hers. "What were you and Mom talking about?"

He shook his head, the movement nearly imperceptible. Then he let her go and disappointment dropped like a weight inside her.

Until he shut the door, turned off the light and walked slowly back to her side.

Chapter Ten

"Logan," she whispered as he pulled her toward him.

He didn't answer. He fitted her against him, bent his head down to her. Pressed his mouth against hers as he cupped the back of her head with his hand. She slipped her arms around him, reveled in the feel of his muscular back.

The darkness of the room enfolded her like a blanket as he slanted his mouth across hers. She wanted to think that they were suspended in time, in space, touched by magic. That anything could happen here, anything permitted. Wanted to pretend there would be no consequences, that she could abandon free will and let Logan take control.

She knew better. Knew that she should stop him now, before his touch overwhelmed her senses. Before pleasure crowded out conscious thought. But after years of constraining herself, years of denying herself intimate human contact, didn't she deserve this moment? Despite the consequences, despite the perilous certainty that she would only be drawn that much closer to Logan.

He shifted, easing himself to the edge of the bed and her into his lap. His hand dove under the pajama top, resting lightly at her waist, moving incrementally slowly up her side. He'd begun to play her mouth with his clever tongue, dipping inside, drawing back, leaving her aching for the wet contact.

She still had time to stop him. As drugging as his kisses were, as breath-stealing as his touch was, she needed only to pull back, to tense her body the slightest bit. He would release her, let her slide from his lap and gain her feet. She could walk out of this room. Yet she relaxed even further into his arms.

His thumb stroked along the underside of her breast, along its curve, the slowness of the motion stealing her breath. Her nipples ached for that same caress, but he continued to tease her, moving just close enough but still out of reach.

The flannel top, which felt so cozy minutes before, now felt hot and constricting. Squirming, she got one hand on the hem and pulled it up. Logan helped her, taking the garment over her head and tossing it to the floor. She welcomed the cool air against her skin, relished the contrast with Logan's searing touch.

She felt him hard and ready against her hip, wanted desperately to feel him inside her. He shifted again, yanking back the covers and pressing her onto the bed. Grabbing a handful of his sweater, she tried to push it up out of the way, but he took her hands and held them loosely above her head. He kissed her again, scalding her with his lips, his tongue.

He trailed his mouth along her jaw, her throat, her collarbone. His tongue blazed a path centered between her breasts, leaving them aching for attention. The fingers of his free hand curled into the elastic waistband of her bottoms, stripping them and her panties off.

Straddling her on his knees, he arched down, his mouth closing finally around her nipple, his tongue laving it. Shani moaned low in her throat at the hot wetness against her sensitive flesh. She thought she'd burst out of her skin at the sensation as it shot from her breast to between her legs, a taut cord of fire.

He tasted her other breast as well, then moved on, along her rib cage, over the slight mound of her belly, to the triangle of curls between her legs. The first puff of his breath against the tender skin of her inner thigh had her squirming on the bed. Devon had never touched her this way, put his mouth anywhere but against her lips or breast. He rarely touched her at all below the waist, except to part her legs to enter her.

Logan eased her legs wider, his thumbs grazing the juncture on either side of those trailing curls. He kissed her gently, his hot breath teasing the swollen, aching flesh. Her hands still above her head, she wrapped her fingers around the wrought-iron of the headboard, the metal cold under her heated palms.

She swallowed back a moan at the first brush of Logan's tongue against her center. Fire crackled along her nerve endings, pushing beyond the boundaries of her body. She couldn't sit still, but didn't dare move away from that incandescent sensation.

As he tasted her again and again, she burned hotter and hotter, air harder to drag into her lungs. She let go of the headboard, reaching down for him, reaching out for something she couldn't grasp. Logan locked his fingers in hers as his tongue dove in over and over, driving her to the edge of insanity, the edge of bliss.

She leaped over the precipice, exploding into paradise. The exquisite sensation rocked through her body, seemingly endless, pulsing and strumming along her skin. She came back to herself by degrees, first aware of Logan's mouth still resting on her, his hands locked in hers, the feel of her naked body against the cool sheets.

Opening her eyes, she looked down at him, pale moonlight glinting in his blue eyes. When she tugged, he moved up to lie alongside her, gathering her into his arms.

Her mind still couldn't grasp the surprise, the suddenness of their intimacy. Her body still trembled in the aftermath. Her emotions lay in a jumble, and as she nestled in the sanctuary of Logan's embrace, she struggled to sort them out.

One bright gem glittered amid the confusion, an overpowering realization that terrified Shani to acknowledge. A consequence to their intimacy she would have never anticipated. She tried to blank her mind from its pull, to deny that the gorgeous treasure had lodged itself in her heart. But it burst into her awareness nonetheless.

I love him.

Somehow during their dinners together, the long talks, the glimpses of tenderness she sometimes caught, she'd moved from grudging respect to tentative friendship to a leap of faith she never expected. It wasn't so much the public face of Logan she'd come to love, but what she sensed lay beneath the surface. The truth of him that he was as yet unwilling to fully show her.

"Logan…" She didn't know what she was about to say, what he might have heard when she spoke his name.

"Damn." He whispered the oath, tension suddenly rippling along his body. "Damn."

"Logan—"

But he pushed away, rising to his feet and switching on a bedside light. "Go back to your sister's room."

Shani pulled the covers up to her chin. "We should talk about this."

"We shouldn't have even done this."

He grabbed her pajamas and dropped them on the bed. A knife of hurt in her chest, Shani fumbled with the buttons on the shirt. As she dressed, he watched her, and she shivered at the intensity of his gaze.

Slipping from the bed, she took a step toward him, hand outstretched. He edged away from her.

"Please." She tried to close the distance between them, but again he stepped out of reach.

"Don't," he rasped out.

Now heat rose in her cheeks, mortification settling as a sour brew in her belly. Tears stung her eyes as she tried to understand how this man could take her to heaven one moment, then cut her off from himself the next.

Why couldn't it have just been physical pleasure between them? Why couldn't she have been like other women, who could enjoy their bodies without the specter of deep emotion intruding? Good Lord, how could she have let herself fall in love with him?

Turning on her heel, she strode from the room, picking up speed as she continued down the hall. She took one look back when she got to Rachael's room. A wedge of light from his open door backlit Logan, silhouetting his tall frame.

For a moment, she considered stalking back down the hall, speaking her mind, confessing her feelings for him. But she wasn't sure she could bear the humiliation. Because he would most certainly rebuff her and break her heart all over again. And it was her own fault, for letting him in when she should have fought tooth and nail to keep him out. How could she have been so stupid?

With the book still lying in Logan's room, she had no choice but to switch off the light and lie in the dark until she fell asleep. But the knot of pain inside her, the endless replay of what had happened with Logan, kept her awake for hours.

For the rest of her visit, Shani did her best to keep the chaos inside her to herself. In conversations with her family, she forced herself to smile and laugh when she really wanted to weep. When she interacted with Logan, she managed to maintain a cool neutrality, friendly on the surface, keeping her emotions well protected.

Her mother, always preternaturally aware of any secrets her daughters harbored, no doubt guessed that something was amiss, but she kept that observation to herself. Still, Shani often saw her mother's considering look pass between Logan and Shani. Somehow, Mrs. Jacoby sensed that something had happened, and whatever it was troubled her.

As much as it grieved her to say goodbye to her sister and mother, Shani felt tremendous relief as she and Logan drove to the airport. She still had the hours traveling beside him, but at least the tension of putting up a front for her family would soon be over. She bought a book at a newsstand in the Eastern Iowa Airport, intending to keep her nose buried in it during both legs of their trip home.

Their conversation was limited to the bare essentials—whether she was warm enough in the car, if she wanted to check her small carry-on or keep it with her. He stayed close to her during their wait in the security line, as they walked to their gate. But his silence weighed heavily on her. She knew they should talk, clear the air about what had happened between them. But she just didn't have the energy to initiate the discussion.

Too wired to sleep on the Iowa-to-Denver flight, she did her best to focus on the book that had sounded so fascinating when she'd looked it over at the newsstand. Logan kept his head bent over his own work, flipping through another stack of documents he'd brought with him. When they got to Denver and learned that a freak snowstorm would delay their flight to Sacramento, Shani almost wept with exhaustion.

Logan took one look at her, then commandeered several in a row of plastic seats near their gate. Spreading out his thick parka, he gestured to the makeshift bed.

"Take a nap," he told her. "I'll watch over you."

That did bring tears to her eyes, although she turned her head away so that Logan wouldn't see. She slept for three-quarters of the two-hour layover, tiredness dragging her into sleep despite the hardness of the plastic chairs she stretched out on.

It was nearly 10:00 p.m. by the time Logan pulled the Mercedes into the gate of his estate, almost midnight Iowa time. Shani could barely see straight as they wound up the drive. When she glanced toward the cottage, it almost looked as if the lights were on inside and the door lay ajar.

Did Logan call Mrs. Singh and ask her to turn down Shani's bed? She didn't recall him calling anyone since they landed, but as fuzzy-brained as she felt, he could have when she wasn't paying attention.

They pulled up to the cottage, and Shani fumbled with her seat belt. When she reached for the door handle, Logan put out his hand to stop her.

"Stay here," he ordered.

"You don't need to open my door for me," she muttered as she pushed the handle.

He grabbed her arm. "Shani, stay here. Lock the door after me."

Fear trilling along her spine, she swung her door shut again and locked it after Logan had slipped out. Focusing on the cottage, she realized the door *was* open and it appeared that most of the lights were on. She suspected it wasn't Mrs. Singh who had left the cottage like that. But who?

Logan cautiously pushed open the door and took a quick look inside. He unclipped his cell phone from his belt. He tapped in three digits—911, Shani guessed.

As he disappeared inside, Shani shivered, looking around her. Could someone still be here, watching? Even inside the locked Mercedes, terror bubbled up inside.

Finally, Logan came outside again. At his gesture, she unlocked the car and joined him on the cottage's small front porch.

He took her hand. "Someone broke in."

Even though she'd guessed as much, the news wrenched her. A sudden realization sent her into a panic. "Where's Seymour? Did he get out? He's always been an indoor cat."

"I found him hiding under the bed," Logan reassured her. "I shut the bedroom door."

At that, Shani burst into tears. Logan folded her into his embrace, letting her soak his sweater with her sobbing. She sagged against him, the last vestige of her energy evaporating. He lifted her in his arms and carried her inside.

A brief survey of the cottage revealed that although the bedroom had been torn apart by the intruder—all the dresser drawers pulled out, the mattress askew on the bed, a lamp tipped and broken—it seemed nothing had been taken. Shani's small jewelry box had been opened, but the few pieces she hadn't taken with her to Iowa were still inside. The television and DVD player in the living room didn't seem to have been moved.

Logan didn't leave Shani's side the entire time they waited for the police. Only after the female deputy from Placer County Sheriff's Department arrived did he hurry over to the main house to check the situation there.

"Nothing's disturbed in the main house," he told the deputy once he'd returned. "Front and back doors still locked, all the windows are intact."

"What happened to your alarm system?" the woman asked.

Shani could see the tautness in Logan's jaw as it worked. "I don't know why the exterior segment of the system didn't pick him up. It looks like we neglected to set the alarm in the cottage before we left on Wednesday."

The deputy looked around her at the general state of disarray. "If I had to guess, I'd say the perpetrator was searching for something. Drawers pulled out and emptied, closet and cupboards rifled through. Yet you say nothing's been stolen…."

"I can't find anything missing," Shani said, sitting on the sofa with Seymour in her lap. The cat clung to her like Velcro, purring loudly.

"Can you think of what someone could have been looking for?" the deputy asked. "Do you keep drugs here?"

Shani shook her head. "Other than the progesterone and estrogen for my pregnancy. I'm guessing that's not what you meant."

"No," the deputy said. "But a druggie probably wouldn't have checked the labels. He would have just taken the bottles."

"They're still in here," Logan said, checking the refrigerator. "Doesn't look like they've been disturbed."

The officer shook her head. "I can send someone from the CSI team down to dust for prints, but that won't do you any good if the perp's not in the system."

After taking down a few more details, the deputy left abruptly when another, more pressing call came in. After the woman had gone, Shani sank back against the sofa, her fingers buried in Seymour's fur. She tried to will herself to stop trembling but couldn't seem to manage it.

Logan stood over her, his face clouded with anger. "You can't stay here any longer."

She nodded. "I'll go back to the apartment."

"Not the apartment. You're moving to the main house."

Shani wordlessly shook her head, but Logan wasn't about to concede this argument. "I can't be sure of your security out here. The apartment's too far away. Unless you'd rather I stay with you there—"

"No. It's too small. We'd be…"

Far too close together. Bad enough in the main house with her bedroom only down the hall from his. But at least Mrs. Singh would be there most of the time.

Logan sat beside her on the sofa, resisting the urge to wrap his arms around her. "Shani…" When she kept her gaze downcast on her cat, he risked placing his fingertips on her cheek, turning her to face him. "I've done a damn poor job of keeping you safe."

"It's not your fault."

"I didn't set the cottage alarm when I should have." A sudden thought punched a hole in his chest. "What if this bastard had broken in while you were here? While you were asleep or during the day when I was at work? The thought of you being alone, unprotected—"

She dropped her hand over his, her simple touch soothing him. "I'll stay in the main house."

He took a long breath. "I'll call Patrick Cade tomorrow. Arrange a more visible security presence at the estate."

Patrick was most well known for the Internet security firm that provided all the software that kept Good Sport's computer network safe. He also owned a more covert business—an executive-protection service that provided bodyguards and security staff for celebrities and CEOs. Logan had never felt the need to utilize Patrick's less-public services until now, but he knew enough about the man to trust anyone in his employ.

Unwilling to let Shani leave his sight, Logan accompanied her into the bedroom as she gathered up some toiletries, a nightshirt and a change of clothes for tomorrow. He took care of tucking the cat into his carrier. Once Logan had Shani safely at the main house, he would come back for whatever other necessities she required. Tomorrow he'd bring the rest of her things over.

As she looked around the bedroom one last time, her foot caught on the nightstand drawer that had been pulled out and dropped on the floor. The drawer was flipped up on its side, spilling what was left of its contents. Logan's hand on Shani's arm prevented her from falling, but couldn't stop her from barking her shin on the drawer.

She sank to the edge of the bed, tears of frustration glittering in her eyes. "This isn't my night, I guess."

"You need to get into bed." The thought of joining her there, of holding her until morning, flickered into his mind.

She started to rise, her gaze downcast. She suddenly dropped to her knees, upending the drawer completely.

"Look," she breathed.

Taped to the bottom of the drawer, up against one of

the edges, was a small key. Shani peeled it off, removing the tape that had affixed it to the drawer.

She held it out to him. "I think it's for Arianna's diary." Angling toward the bed, she lifted the skirt and slid her hand between the mattress and box spring.

She sighed, relief clear in the sound. A moment later, she produced Arianna's diary. "I can't imagine anyone would be searching for this, but I was a little afraid it might be gone."

As she tried to get her feet under her, she swayed and sat back down. Taking her hand, Logan lifted her, wrapping his arm around her waist. "It's past midnight. You can open the diary in the morning."

With the cat carrier in one hand and Shani nestled on his other side, they made their way to the main house. Over Shani's objections, Logan carried her upstairs to one of the guest rooms that Mrs. Singh always kept ready. He brought the cat up next, then ordered Shani to change and get into bed while he carried their luggage and a last few things over from the cottage.

By the time he delivered the last load—her textbooks and book bag—Shani had already fallen asleep. She'd left the bedside light on and he could see the shadows under her eyes. A consequence of the shock of the break-in, surely, but he felt a certain responsibility for some of the stress reflected in her face. His complete lapse in judgment Thanksgiving night had shaken the delicate balance they'd achieved in their relationship.

He sat on the edge of the bed, gently so as not to disturb her. If he couldn't curl up beside her, curve his body against hers, he would allow himself a few minutes to watch her sleep. As her mother had said, Shani nurtured a precious gift inside her. He couldn't help but want to be with her, ponder that life growing within.

Except it was more than that. The realization of how vulnerable Shani was, pregnant with his child, how horrifying it had been to imagine her endangered by the SOB that had broken into the cottage went beyond her being a surrogate mother for him. Somewhere along the line, she had become as important to him as the child she would bear.

Yet, after the baby was born, when the surrogacy agreement had been fulfilled, she would walk out of his life. There would be no reason for them to have any contact at all. Despite her relationship with Arianna, Shani had been a near stranger to him before last August and would become one again.

As he imagined Shani leaving his home that last time, despair took root inside him. How could he possibly let her go? Never see her again?

Mrs. Jacoby's words echoed in his mind as they had so often since Thanksgiving. *What would it hurt if you married her?* He hadn't answered her that night, presented any argument. But now, as he watched Shani sleep, he couldn't hide from the truth.

How miserable he'd made his wife in their marriage, how unhappy she'd been. How unbearable it would be if he ruined Shani's life as he had Arianna's. How he would be as helpless to make Shani happy as he had been his late wife.

What would it hurt? Shani, certainly. And perhaps their child, as well, subjected as he would be to the inevitable tension between his parents.

Still, the notion had sunk its teeth into him deeply. It was never far from his conscious thoughts these days. If he was selfish enough to ignore the emotional fallout for Shani, he could have everything he wanted by marrying her. He would keep her by his side. His child would have a mother, an extended family.

He could make love to her every night. Just the thought set him on fire.

For a moment, he let himself relive Thanksgiving night, when he'd given in to the burning need to see her climax. It had been a shock to every cell in his body watching her, her ecstasy nearly as satisfying as his own would have been. It astonished him that her pleasure had been enough for him.

He wanted her even now. He wanted to push up that T-shirt she slept in, discover whether she wore anything else in that warm bed. Touch her all over—her mouth, her breasts, the cleft of her thighs. Bring her over the edge, then push inside her and feel her constrict around him as she came again.

If he married her, he could do that—touch her, make love to her, create more children with her after this one. Wake up every morning with her in his bed. Make a life with her.

Could he make a better marriage with Shani? She and Arianna were different women. Would he do it right this time, make Shani happy as he'd never been able to with Arianna? Would he see when Shani was overtaken by sorrow as he hadn't with Arianna? And would he know the right thing to say, the right thing to do?

Or would he fumble through their marriage just as he had with Arianna? Would Shani end up as despondent as his late wife had been? Because of him, because he had no real competence as a husband?

He'd wanted so desperately to love his wife, to give that love to her in a way that she would feel it, acknowledge it. But in all their years of marriage, he'd never learned the knack of love. Maybe it was buried deep inside him, sparked somewhere in his heart, but he never seemed to have the capacity to build the bridge between himself and Arianna.

He might wish otherwise, but there was no logical reason to think it would be different with Shani. Their relationship, although less awkward than it had been at the outset, was still uneasy much of the time. He sensed that she respected him, at times even liked him. But love—that wasn't any part of the equation. He only knew he couldn't let her go.

Shani stirred, squeezing her eyes more tightly shut, as if the light of the bedside lamp disturbed her sleep. Logan quickly snapped it off, then stood over her in the darkness. He couldn't see her now, but he could hear her breathe, smell her unique fragrance. He wanted to stand there all night just to be near her.

But he forced himself to go to his own room, ready himself for bed, crawl wearily under the covers. He shut off his mind with ruthless efficiency, all but ordered himself to sleep.

The next morning, the nurse arrived at eight to administer Shani's injections. While she and Shani shared a laughter-filled conversation over Shani's relief that the injections would be finished in ten days, Logan made his call to Patrick Cade. They set up an appointment for later that day to meet. Then he had to leave a message with a locksmith Patrick recommended who worked on Sundays.

While Shani finished her breakfast, Logan tried to relax on the living room sofa with the paper, but nothing he read made any sense. Again and again, he lifted his gaze to Shani, as she smiled at the comics, took a sip of her herbal tea, nibbled on the last of her bagel. He stared, obsessed with her, rapt at every detail of her face, her every movement.

Then she turned toward him, her gaze meeting his. Her lips parted as if he'd surprised her, her breath seeming to catch in her throat. His chest ached as he watched her. And he realized that no matter how selfish it might be, he couldn't let her go. One way or another, he would tie her to him.

He dropped the newspaper, crushed it under his foot as he rose and started toward the dining room. She watched him warily as he approached, stood over her.

"Don't say no," he said, his voice shaking.

Now she looked even more alarmed. "What?"

Still he plowed ahead. "Will you give some thought to what I have to say?"

"I…" Her brow furrowed. "Yes."

He took a breath. "Marry me."

Chapter Eleven

For several moments, Shani couldn't muster a coherent thought to frame a reply. She'd heard the words *marry me,* but they made so little sense coming from Logan's mouth that she assumed she'd misinterpreted him. She kept replaying the last few seconds, hoping she could somehow clarify what he'd said.

She shook her head in incomprehension. "Why would I marry you?"

Except, she knew the answer, had locked it up inside her. Despite her determination to keep the truth hidden, heat flagged her cheeks. She took another sip of tea to cover her inner turmoil.

Thankfully, he couldn't read her mind, didn't catch the significance of the color in her face. He ticked off a list of rationalizations for matrimony as if describing employee benefits to a company new-hire.

"No money worries, ever again. Stay home with the

baby as long as you like, then a guarantee of an excellent job at Good Sport when you're ready. You can work part-time or full-time. Or go back to school for your MBA."

"We barely know each other, Logan. Even still, even after…" Images from Thanksgiving night flashed through her mind.

He pulled out a chair and sat close to her. "We both have an interest in what's best for that child you're carrying. You can't tell me you don't care about the baby."

"Of course I care." She cared far too much, more than she should.

"You know as well as I do, a child does best with two parents, something neither of us had ourselves. Wouldn't you want to give this baby more than what we had?"

Treacherous hope blossomed inside her and she shut it down ruthlessly. "This is your baby, Logan."

His hands cradled her face. "But it could be yours, too."

Say yes! her heart screamed. *You love the baby already. You love—*

"No." Shoving back her chair, she sprang to her feet, put the table between her and Logan. "You don't—we don't love each other."

He rose, turning away from her. "We'll talk about this later." He walked from the room, and a few moments later, she heard the slam of the front door.

She rewound the last few minutes in her mind, dilemma resting heavily on her shoulders. How could she say yes? How could she possibly say no?

Logan ran down the front porch steps, then took off along the path toward the cottage, his agitation increasing with each step. He moved faster as he passed the cottage, breaking into a jog, then a flat-out run up the leaf-strewn rise toward the back of his property. He didn't stop until he reached the back fence, leaning against the six-foot stuccoed concrete barrier as he gasped for breath.

Of course, he'd bungled it. Where he should have used finesse to bring Shani around to agreement about marriage, he'd stumbled in like a ham-handed idiot. When he should have been sensitive to how much she'd been through the past several days, not to mention the welcome-home last night, he'd presented their marriage to her as if it were some kind of prospective business deal.

He struck the stout concrete wall with his fist, grazing his knuckles on the hard surface. Drawing blood got him nowhere, just further demonstrated his thickheadedness. Still, he pounded the wall again before he pushed off to walk along its perimeter.

He should have anticipated the subject of love would come up, should have had an answer ready. Would it have been enough to tell her simply that he didn't want her to leave him? That she'd become a part of his life? Or would that have meant nothing if he couldn't tell her he loved her?

As he strode along the perimeter of his property, the November cold cut through the long-sleeved Henley and khakis he'd pulled on that morning. The soles of his loafers skidded in the mud hidden beneath the leaf fall from the oaks. If he'd had a brain in his head, he would have grabbed a jacket before he'd run outside. But where Shani was concerned, he couldn't seem to think clearly.

When he tripped on a fallen limb hidden in the brush and nearly stumbled to his knees, he stopped his headlong rush. Easing himself onto the stump of a black oak that had been felled when he'd had the wall built, he forced himself to regain some self-control.

He couldn't lie to her, promise to offer her a love match when he couldn't find those feeling inside him.

He had to hope she could be satisfied with everything else he could give her—support, faithfulness, physical love when she was ready for it. She would never want for anything, and she would be the mother of his child.

He would have to convince her that that would be enough.

Using the wall to push to his feet again, he glimpsed something out of the corner of his eye. He climbed on the stump to get a better look at the capped top of the wall. A torn swatch of fabric was stuck to the rough stucco, a dark stain that could have been blood near it. When he levered himself up over the top of the wall, he saw footprints in a patch of bare mud on the other side. Marks that could have been from a ladder bracketed the footprints.

A chill coursed down his spine. Their intruder had accessed the estate here. The adjacent property was still undeveloped, with only a three-wire fence delineating its perimeter. Easy enough to access from the road.

That explained how he'd been able to foil the exterior motion detector. In this part of the property, the previous owner had deactivated a segment of the circuit—too many deer and raccoons setting off the alarms. Logan had been lulled into a false sense of security when he'd had the six-foot wall built. He'd let the deficiency slip his mind. That would be the first thing he'd have Patrick rectify.

A sudden urgency flooded Logan. He had to check on Shani, to assure himself she was safe. He cursed the fact that his meeting with Patrick wouldn't be until this afternoon. Because he hadn't wanted to leave Shani alone, he had to wait for Mrs. Singh's return. He wouldn't be able to get a man on-site to increase the estate's protection until this evening at the earliest.

Dodging through the trees, he trotted back down the

hill toward the house. He'd only been gone twenty minutes or so; nothing could have happened to Shani in such a short period of time. Nevertheless, he had to be sure, had to see her with his own eyes.

He shouted her name the moment he pushed open the front door. She didn't answer. A quick perusal told him she wasn't downstairs. He took the stairs two at a time, breathing heavily as he reached her room. He pounded on the door, his knuckles stinging where he'd scraped them.

Pressing his ear to the door, he listened for footsteps. Nothing. He pounded again, harder, terror surging inside him. He tried to tell himself she might be sleeping or in the shower. Except he couldn't hear the shower running and he doubted she'd be napping already after having woken only a few hours ago.

"Shani!" he shouted, pounding a third time, his hand on the knob ready to open the door.

Finally he heard her footsteps. He backed away, realizing he'd probably scare the wits out of her if he didn't reel in his irrational fear.

As it was, he had to use all his self-control to avoid grabbing her and pulling her into his arms the instant he saw her face. He made a focused effort to regulate his breathing as he swiped damp palms on his khakis.

"You didn't answer," he blurted out.

"I was going over next week's reading." Her wariness had returned.

He considered pouring out everything that had been running through his mind in the past several minutes, every argument, every persuasion. If he just said exactly the right words in exactly the right way, surely she'd agree.

He realized his frame of mind was too undisciplined, and if he let it all spill out, he would make a hash of his well-reasoned case for marriage. He had to give himself time to regroup before he brought up the discussion again.

He dropped his gaze to his feet, casting about for something to justify interrupting her. "Since I haven't heard back from the locksmith yet, I want to clear the rest of your things from the cottage. Did you want to come with me or should I take care of it myself?"

She stared at him, considering, as the seconds ticked by. "I'll help you." She edged past him through the door.

"Let me grab a few boxes from the garage," he told her as they reached the foot of the stairs.

"I'll meet you over at the cottage, then." She started for the door.

"No, wait!" His tone earned him a sharp look from her. He didn't want to tell her about his discovery of the intruder's entry point until he had one of Patrick's men in place. "Just stay here. I'll be right back."

He quickly retrieved the boxes and was relieved to see Shani had waited.

He set the boxes aside on the sofa. "Before we head over, I want to show you how the alarm system works for the main house and the exterior circuit."

He ran her through the activation procedure, explaining the different codes for interior and exterior security. After she'd activated and deactivated the system twice, he felt confident she could handle it on her own.

He collected the cardboard boxes and they left the house for the cottage. "Even once I have one of Patrick's men on-site, when you're home alone, or when it's just you and Mrs. Singh, I want the exterior system activated. I can deactivate it at the gate when I return."

He thought she might argue, but she just nodded. "I'm guessing there isn't much the police will be able to do about the break-in."

"Since nothing was taken, it's not high priority."

He stepped in front of her before she reached the cottage door, pushing it open. Blocking her from entering, he made a quick check of the interior.

He moved aside and followed her into the bedroom. "Anything heavy, I'll carry. You're not to pick up anything until I check the weight first."

She rolled her eyes at him, then lowered herself to the floor with one of the boxes. Logan unhooked blouses, skirts and slacks from the closet rod and lay the pile of clothes on the bed. The closet empty, he opened the top dresser drawer.

Shani jumped to her feet. "I'll do that."

She took his arm and started to pull him away from the dresser, but not before he'd filled his hand with a collection of dainty panties that had been neatly folded inside. She tried to take them from him, but he found himself mesmerized by the silky texture, the bright colors of the scraps of satin and lace. Arianna had mostly worn conservative cotton underwear. Shani seemed to have a preference for silk.

It was all he could do to keep from holding them up against his face, to feel their smooth texture against his skin. Thanksgiving night, he'd stripped her of a pair just like these, but he'd been so focused on baring her body, he'd swept her panties aside without looking at them.

Now he wanted her to model every pair. Maybe starting with the midnight-blue with its small satin bow or the scarlet with lace edging. How would it feel to run his finger slowly along the elastic waist, to tug that silky nothing from her hips, down her long legs?

"Please," she said, squeezing his arm harder until he released her unmentionables.

As she turned he spotted the color in her cheeks.

Because he'd embarrassed her? Or maybe because some of the same thoughts had raced through her mind?

He'd damn well better rein in his rampant imagination. "Should I clear out the other drawers?"

"The bottom three are…safe." She dumped a load of panties into an empty box. "T-shirts, sweaters, some sweatpants."

He'd thought her outerwear would be less provocative, but no matter what of Shani's he touched, his mind wandered into dangerous territory. Because a T-shirt would make him think of the bra underneath. He could push that T-shirt up, expose a delicate lacy bra like the one Shani had just dropped into the box with the panties. Then he'd unhook the bra, slide the straps down her arms, pull it away from her small, perfect breasts.

He slammed shut the last empty drawer. "Ready to take the first load over?"

"Sure." Her voice trembled, the soft sound stroking along his nerve endings.

She reached for the nearest box, but he leaned in to pull it away. His arm brushed against hers and he could barely induce himself to break the contact.

He lifted the box, assured himself that with its contents of lacy silk, it weighed only a pound or so. He slid it back over toward Shani, then hefted the heavy hanging clothes from the bed.

They retraced their steps back toward the house, Shani clutching the box close to her chest. "Mrs. Singh will be back today?"

"Around three. She'll make us dinner."

In the guest room, he put away the hanging clothes, keeping his eyes off Shani as she loaded the intimates in the dresser. His gaze fell on the diary sitting on the nightstand.

"Have you read any of it?" he asked.

"What?" She turned, saw the direction of his gaze. "No. I thought I ought to get some work done before I take the time for the diary." She set aside the empty box. "Did you want to see it?"

He walked over toward the bed, ran his fingers over the fine leather of the diary's cover. Arianna rarely wrote in the journal while in his presence. That was likely intentional. She was probably reluctant to share those inner thoughts.

He shook his head. "I don't think I should."

"She's gone, Logan," Shani said quietly. "It won't matter to her anymore."

He looked up at Shani. "I'm not sure I want to know."

After their conversation about the diary, Shani found it difficult to think about anything else. She took one more trip to the cottage with Logan to bring over a small box of toiletries, then left the remainder of the toting to him. She planted herself at the desk in the guest room, her industrial organization book open in front of her, but between her anticipation of Logan returning with the last load and the tantalizing diary sitting on the nightstand, she comprehended little of what she read.

Even still, she kept doggedly at her reading, switching to her principles of marketing text and slogging her way through until her stomach protested that it was lunchtime. When she headed downstairs, she was relieved to discover that Logan was holed up in his office, his voice carrying through the partially open door. She managed to slap together a sandwich in the kitchen and hurry upstairs again with her plate and glass of milk without being seen.

After wolfing down her sandwich and gulping down

her milk, she opened her marketing book again, but couldn't resist the siren call of the diary. Rising from the desk, she nudged off her sneakers and padded over to the bed. With the key tucked into the spine of the diary where she'd left it, she climbed on the bed and sat cross-legged against the pillows.

Fishing the key from the spine, she set the book on the bed in front of her. What if Logan was right, that there might be something in this slim volume that Shani wouldn't want to know? What if there were secrets in here that best remained hidden?

Then she would keep them to herself. She didn't have to share anything with Logan from these pages. He had as much as told her he'd just as soon not know.

Logan had brought over the portrait of Arianna as a girl, had propped it on top of the dresser with a promise to hang it later. The girl Arianna had been gazed down at Shani, her smile sweet and wistful. Shani wished she could ask that girl if she was doing the right thing by opening the Pandora's box of Arianna's past.

Should I? Shani asked, the key in the palm of her hand.

Go ahead, she imagined Arianna answering. *I trust you with my secrets.*

Shani slipped the key neatly into the lock, a perfect fit. Turning it, she released the strap and opened the book.

Chapter Twelve

It fell open, not in the middle, but about two-thirds in where several pages had been torn out. The remainder of the diary after those torn pages was blank. There were no loose sheets tucked anywhere else in the journal.

Setting aside that puzzle, Shani flipped to the front of the diary, where Arianna had written her name and a date—about two-and-a-half years before her death. Shani turned over the flyleaf, opening to the first hand-written page.

This may be a hopeless cause, but the therapist insists it will help. I don't see how mulling over my constant grief will make it go away, but I'm willing to try.

Shani didn't remember Arianna ever mentioning a therapist, but as private as she was about some things, it wasn't a surprise her friend would keep that quiet. In those last two years, there *had* been some moments of bright-ness, so maybe Arianna's time in counseling had helped.

I have tried, throughout my marriage, to blame my unhappiness on my husband and his failings. But if I am to believe the therapist, neither my happiness nor unhappiness are his responsibility. Only my own.

So many conversations with Arianna had centered on Logan, the things he'd said or not said, things he'd done or not done. The business trip he'd taken on their tenth anniversary. The gift of a bracelet when she'd told him she wanted earrings. The fact that during their sixteen-year marriage Logan rarely told Arianna, "I love you," and when he did, it seemed forced and insincere.

And yet—he'd taken Arianna out for a lavish celebratory dinner just a few days after their anniversary. He'd later given her the earrings, custom-made and a perfect match for the bracelet. And there were the cards, presented unexpected, that said on paper what he couldn't seem to say aloud.

At the time, the way Arianna described it through the dark-colored lens of her life, it seemed Logan was incapable of affection toward his wife unless prodded and pushed. But now, knowing him better, looking back over the ways he'd tried to make Shani's life comfortable, how he'd so willingly given his time to help her with school, she wondered how accurate that picture of Logan had been.

Shani continued to read, flipping past pages filled with the mundane and the sorrowful, stopping at another written about a month after the first entry.

Was I ever happy in our marriage? Good God, have I ever been happy at all? There must have been times, there had to be. But the older I've gotten, the more my world has closed in on me. The more I've focused on grief. I'm so terrified to hope for something good, to

*count on joy. Because the moment I do, it will all fall
apart, leaving me in a nightmare.*

The words stunned Shani. She hadn't realized how
dark Arianna's life had been. When they spent time
together, Shani had seen sorrow in her friend's eyes, but
she'd still laughed, shared jokes. Glossed over her complaints at times, at others cried in Shani's arms.

Never knowing better, Shani had placed all the blame
on Logan. Had assumed Arianna's cold, distant husband
had created the sadness in his wife. But that bleakness
had been there from the start. Even in the girl in the
portrait, with her wistful smile, but sad eyes.

Shani read on, Arianna's struggles revealed page by
page. Apparently the therapist had recommended medication several times, but Arianna had refused. Still, near
the end of the written pages, there was a sense Arianna
was climbing out of the abyss.

Maybe there are *different ways to show love. Maybe
some of what Logan does is his way of trying to please me.
Maybe I have more to do with his failures than he does.*

Shani flipped to the last entry, just before the torn-
out pages. Only one line written there—*Three more
e-mails today—should I tell him?* Shani fanned through
the remainder of the diary, searching for anything
further, and came up empty.

Tell who? It had to be Logan. But tell him what?
Could she have met someone, was she having an affair?
She never gave Shani so much as a hint that that was
happening, but obviously Arianna kept plenty to herself.
Could that have been the source of her occasional lighter
mood the last few months before she died?

Shani shut the diary, locking it again and tucking it
into the nightstand drawer. She had no business specu-
lating on Arianna's enigmatic question. As curious as

Shani was, the truth behind what her friend had written was better left laid to rest just as Arianna was.

But what about the other insights—that Arianna had started to see Logan as a good man despite the cool facade. That as clumsy as his demonstrations of affection had sometimes been, he'd given his best to his wife. That maybe with time, they might have made a happier marriage.

Shifting on the bed, Shani tugged aside the comforter and lay back against the pillows. Arianna's words eddied through her mind, reshaping her thoughts, breaking down and rebuilding the foundation of what she thought she understood. She needed time to process this, to see how to cope with this reshaping of her world.

Snapping off the bedside light, she eased herself under the comforter, willing herself to relax. She needed a nap, to rest her body, to shut down her conscious mind. Then she would know where to go from here.

Logan walked out of Patrick Cade's El Dorado Hills office, relieved for the first time since the discovery of the break-in Saturday night. He'd already called Mrs. Singh to alert her to the imminent arrival of one of Patrick's men, a no-nonsense ex-marine with an impeccable résumé. He asked Mrs. Singh to pass the information along to Shani, then after he hung up, nearly called back to speak with Shani himself. Even though he'd be home again in less than an hour, would be sharing dinner with her. After not having seen her all afternoon, he felt an urgent need to hear the sound of her voice.

He put his preoccupation with Shani aside and focused on the afternoon's next meeting. His attorney, John Evans, had agreed to see him at Evans's home in Fair Oaks on a Sunday. Despite Shani's refusal of his marriage proposal, Logan wanted to clarify some legal issues in the event he could persuade her otherwise. In particular, the surrogacy agreement she'd signed stipulated that Shani had no rights to the child she carried. Logan wanted to know if, should they marry, Shani would have to adopt the baby or if they could rescind the earlier document.

His cell rang just as he exited Highway 50 at Sunrise. At the stoplight, he made a quick check of caller ID. Not Shani, he noted, disappointment knotting in his stomach. Even worse, it was his father.

Pressing the answer button on his earpiece, he continued north on Sunrise. "What's up?"

"Not much," his father answered, his voice slightly raspy in Logan's ear. "How's that little bun doing?"

Alarms clanged in Logan's head. It had been just over a week since his dad had called last. Colin Rafferty never called more frequently than once a month.

"What do you want, Dad?" Logan asked warily.

"Can't a father just call to talk?"

He turned right on Sunset, then pulled into a strip mall parking lot to focus on the phone call. "How much do you need this time?"

"Who says I need money?"

Logan rubbed at his temple. "I transferred funds to you ten days ago. Have you gone through it already?"

His father didn't answer. After several long moments of silence, Logan wondered if his cell had lost the signal. "Dad?"

"When's that kid due, anyway?" The rasp in his father's voice seemed more pronounced.

"Early June." Unease prickled up Logan's spine.

"Did I ever tell you what a loudmouth you were as a baby? You'd wake up at o'dark-thirty screaming your head off. I'd wear a track in the carpet trying to quiet you down."

His father had walked him at night when he'd been an infant? Impossible to believe. More likely Colin Rafferty had done it once and embroidered the memory into a more frequent occurrence.

And yet…Logan had a dim recollection of a photograph of himself as a baby, bright eyes wide open, head nestled on his father's shoulder. "Sorry you lost sleep over me." Logan instantly regretted the harsh edge to his tone.

"Your mother couldn't soothe you." The rough whisper was barely audible. "And she was dead tired. So I'd tuck you against my chest, walk you back and forth in the moonlight."

Logan softened inside at the mental picture. He knew better—this was the same man who was never home throughout Logan's childhood, who had left him with a neighbor's nanny for a week after his mother died. Not the revisionist loving father Colin Rafferty tried to evoke now.

It didn't matter anymore. "What did you want, Dad?" Logan asked again. "If it's money, you'll have to wait until tomorrow."

"I don't need a damn thing," Colin said, although there was no heat in his words, despite the expletive. "I have to go."

The phone disconnected, leaving Logan staring down at his cell. He hadn't had a conversation with his father that hadn't involved money in fifteen years or more. As Logan's fortunes rose and Colin Rafferty's sank, his dad's requests for just a little to get him by had grown with each contact.

And why the sudden interest in the baby, after he'd chided Logan for going through with the surrogacy at all? Logan tried to suss out what scheme his father might be hatching that his grandchild-to-be might provide leverage for, but he came up empty.

Stopping to talk to his father had made Logan late for his appointment with his attorney. Pulling back out into traffic, Logan continued on his way, redirecting his attention to his upcoming meeting. Whatever his father's game was, Logan would just have to deal with it when the time came. No point in wasting energy on it now when he had much more important issues to handle.

As November came to a close, Shani remained on edge waiting for Logan to bring up the subject of marriage again. If she'd been sure of what her answer would be, she might have brought it up herself just to clear the air. But as she reread Arianna's diary again and again, late at night when she should have been asleep, as she spent her days with Logan and felt her love for him growing, she became more and more confused as to what to do.

But two weeks after he'd made his proposal, he still hadn't revisited it. When they went to dinner to celebrate her twelfth week, the point at which her injections ended and her pregnancy would proceed as any normal pregnancy would, Shani thought he would take that opportunity. He didn't.

December kicked off its increasingly shorter days with an Alaskan cold front that frosted the rooftops and the lawns with white. With finals looming, they spent the weekend indoors, Logan quizzing Shani in the areas she felt she needed to review the most. All the while, the expectation perched on her shoulder that he'd bring the discussion around to marriage. By Sunday afternoon, two weeks before Christmas, he still hadn't.

As if that stress wasn't enough, an air of sensuality

overlaid every word, every look, every interaction between them. As aware of her body as the pregnancy made her, she felt Logan's presence turn up the volume until she could barely think of anything else. If not for his constant patient drilling of the material from her textbooks, none of it would have adhered to a single brain cell. She would walk into her finals a blathering idiot.

As Shani brooded in the kitchen over a cup of decaf Earl Grey, Mrs. Singh called Logan into the living room for a quiet conference. Shani had been grateful for the woman's presence over the weekend. Besides the delectable meals Logan's housekeeper had served up, Mrs. Singh provided a buffer between Shani and Logan. If Mrs. Singh hadn't been there, Shani might have thrown herself at Logan by now, torn off his clothes and dragged him off to the bedroom.

Which would have been horrifying, considering Logan's apparent indifference to her. Maybe that episode on Thanksgiving had been enough for him to decide she really wasn't his type after all. He'd kept his distance since then, touching her only to help her in and out of the car when they went out to dinner, or when their fingers brushed accidentally when he passed her the bread basket. She seemed to be the only one who sensed the electricity that crackled between them.

Logan returned to the breakfast bar where Shani sat with her tea. "Mrs. Singh is going over to Fairfield tonight to babysit her grandsons. She'll be back in the morning."

Every nerve in Shani's body went on full alert. "Did you want to go out to dinner?" she asked in what she hoped was an ordinary tone of voice.

"I'd rather stay in." Logan leaned against the other side of the breakfast bar, his hands gripping the edge of the black granite countertop. "I wanted to get some work done."

His tone was dry, neutral. His expression bland, his eyes unreadable. What seemed momentous to Shani—that she and Logan would be alone in the house—apparently concerned him not at all.

Then her gaze fell to those strong hands, fingers curled around the edge of the counter. She saw the tendons popping out in sharp relief, the rigidity of his arms, the taut way he held his shoulders. When she lifted her gaze to his face again, she caught a glimpse of what he probably didn't want her to see—a searing, barely banked fire.

"Dinner at home would be fine." She could scarcely speak. "Maybe something easy, like omelets."

"Sure." He pushed off from the counter. "Excuse me."

He walked off in the direction of Mrs. Singh's room. A few minutes later, they came through the kitchen, Logan carrying the housekeeper's overnight bag. Shani doubted the sturdy woman, who regularly toted heavy sacks of groceries and laundry baskets, needed help out with her suitcase. Likely, Logan needed something to keep his hands occupied.

Shani certainly did. She rinsed her cup and set it in the dishwasher, then went into the dining room where she and Logan had been working. Stacking her textbooks, she carried them upstairs to her room.

A quick glimpse out the window told her Mrs. Singh was about to pull out through the gate. Then the front door slammed shut. Shani stepped out of her bedroom and to the railing of the landing. Logan, still by the door, looked up at her.

He started up the stairs. Her heart pounding in her ears, Shani struggled to breathe as he approached. One hand still on the rail for support, she turned as he took the last few steps and drew near.

He stood over her, millimeters between them. "I've tried to keep my hands off you," he whispered, "wanted to give you the space to think about my proposal."

She nodded, not quite able to muster her voice. The heat in his eyes burned her to her core.

But still he didn't touch her. "I didn't want sex getting in the way. Didn't want it to be part of your decision."

"Don't you think it should be?" The challenge in the words shocked her. She stunned herself even more when she reached for him, pressing her hand against his cheek and bringing him down to kiss her.

Eyes shut, she absorbed multiple sensations—his skin against her palm, roughened by the day's growth of beard, his mouth stroking across hers, his tongue tracing along the seam of her lips. His hands, one at her waist, the other cupped behind her head. His chest, warm under the T-shirt he wore, the ridge of his response pressing against the vee of her legs.

The weeks since he'd brought her to climax in her mother's house had honed her desire to an exquisite edge. She wanted everything at once—his hands everywhere on her body, and hers on his. His mouth tasting her again. Him settling in the cradle of her legs and entering her.

Logan plunged his tongue into her mouth, his hand at the small of her back fitting her against him. She would have dragged him down onto the carpeted landing, she had so little self-control in that moment. He let her drag his shirt from the waist of his jeans, to slide her hands underneath the knit, but when she tried to push it up and off, he eased away and lifted her into his arms.

She felt dizzy as he carried her down the hall toward his room, light-headed with arousal. He laid her on his bed, standing over her, chest rising and falling as he dragged air into his lungs. His gaze on her felt as palpable as his touch. Her body responded, sensation pooling between her thighs, her nipples growing tight and aching.

Then he leaned over and pushed up her T-shirt, tugging it off. With slow deliberation, he unbuttoned her jeans, lowered the zipper, peeled them from her hips, down her legs. He slipped off her shoes one by one, then tossed shoes and jeans aside.

She shivered as cool air eddied on her heated skin, gooseflesh rising where her body wasn't covered by the teal bra and panties she wore. Sitting on the edge of the bed, Logan pressed his mouth against her belly and rested his rough cheek there.

"When will I feel the baby move?" he asked, his mouth stroking her as he spoke.

"A month or two. It doesn't feel like much—" she sucked in a breath in response to his kisses "—at first. Just a fluttering."

"I can't wait." Another kiss, this one along the elastic of her panties. "Arianna never…"

He didn't have to finish. Shani knew her friend's pregnancy didn't last long enough for her to feel the baby's movement.

Shani shivered again and Logan had to feel it under his mouth. "You're cold. Let me pull down the covers."

She edged aside so he could strip back the bedding. She gasped at the first touch of skin against cool linen.

She smiled up at him. "I need your help warming these sheets."

He undressed quickly, climbing under the covers with her. His heat soaked into her immediately, the hard evidence of his arousal burning against her hip. She couldn't lie still feeling him beside her.

His arms around her, he kissed her, feathery touches with his mouth on hers, then across her cheek, along her jaw, down her throat. He fitted one leg between hers, the firm muscles of his thigh pressing against her sensitized center. She felt damp and hot, her body dancing on the edge of paradise.

His mouth's lazy exploration moved lower, along her collarbone, her sternum, the first softness of her breast. His tongue followed that languid path, leaving fire in its wake, enfolding her world in sensation.

Her body went rigid at the first touch of his tongue on her nipple. As he circled the tautening flesh, he wet the silky knit of her bra, and bliss lapped at her with each concentric touch. At the same time, his hand crept under her panties, leisurely moving through the curls beneath them, dipping between her soft folds. Touching her impossibly heated flesh.

She climaxed with a cry of triumph, her body arching in that moment of ecstasy. Her fingers dug so deeply into his back, a dim part of her wondered at the marks she'd leave behind. Then another wash of rapture swept her away, obliterating awareness of anything but her own body.

By slow degrees, she came back to herself, to Logan lying beside her. She pulled in a breath to speak. "You can't make me leave you this time."

"No," he said softly.

"I want you," she whispered, her hands moving down his body.

He eased from her enough to pull off her panties and bra, then parted her legs to kneel between them. He hesitated there, staring down at her, and for an instant,

Shani thought she saw something in his eyes, the same secret she'd locked in her own heart.

For that moment, she let herself believe that he loved her just as she loved him. That he feared giving that love just as she did. That if she only uttered the words, revealed everything she held inside, he would answer in kind.

But then the ephemeral message vanished, if it had ever been there at all. He lowered his body and with one swift thrust entered her. Climax struck her almost immediately, abandoning her to feelings beyond anything she'd felt before. With her body still reeling from that undistilled joy, another peak hit her, drowning her in an ocean of delight.

He came in tandem with her, groaning, shuddering as he thrust into her. Gasping for breath, he rolled to one side, taking her with him, holding her tight in his arms.

She felt close to tears but pushed them back, afraid he would misinterpret her joy. She burned to tell him the truth, but knew her heart would be at stake if she did. So she lay there in silence, grateful for the intimacy, even if it was only physical.

He eased back from her, locked his gaze with hers. "I won't let you go, Shani."

Shock ran through her at the resolution in his tone. "What do you want, Logan?" She knew, but she wanted to hear him say it again.

He pressed his hand against her cheek. "Marry me."

An hour ago, she might have still refused. But the world had changed. Her answer had suddenly sprung into crystal clarity. No matter what the consequences, what she might pay in heartache, she would take the gift of their legal union.

"Yes." She laid her hand over his, reveling in its warmth against her face. "I'll marry you."

The intensity of his gaze held her tight. "Before... you wanted love, Shani. Nothing's changed."

She bit back her pain. "I know," she said softly.

His thumb drifted across her cheek. "I'll give you everything."

Except love. He didn't have to speak the words out loud. She heard the implication.

Then he took her into his arms again, kissing her, touching her, pulling her back into that maelstrom of passion. Even as she cried out wordlessly in climax, she shouted her love for him silently. It might not be everything she wanted, but to be part of his life, to be able to love him would be enough.

Chapter Thirteen

As a girl, when she'd dreamed of her wedding, she'd imagined a white dress with a ten-foot train one of her young cousins would have had to carry. All her family would be there—all her aunts and uncles, her cousins, her sister standing beside her as maid of honor, her mother with proud tears in her eyes in the front row. Until he left them, her father had been part of the fantasy as well, her hand on his arm as he walked her up the aisle.

The groom had been changeable—Jimmy Wallace in fourth grade, Ben Fisk in sixth. Throughout high school, she auditioned in her mind three or four other possibilities, mentally fitting them into that handsome black tux. The only common thread among them—they loved her passionately, forever and ever.

Then reality arrived in the form of Logan Rafferty.

That Sunday afternoon and evening after she'd

agreed to marry him, she and Logan spent as much time in his bed as out of it. They made love again and again, then lay in each other's arms, quietly making plans for the wedding. They agreed on New Year's Day over omelets quickly thrown together in the kitchen, briefly discussing a guest list before hurrying back upstairs to explore each other's bodies again.

She slept with him that night, but he didn't suggest she move into his room. The next night she went upstairs without him to sleep alone. After that, he kept his distance, as if their lovemaking had never happened. Except the heat in his gaze when he didn't know she was looking at him told a different story.

Once he had her agreement, Logan seemed to want to lock in her decision with a hasty marriage, and there was no dissuading him.

The weekend after Rachael's winter break began, Logan flew Shani's mother and sister out to California. He would have arranged for the rest of the family to attend as well, but Shani told him she wanted the ceremony to be small. Maybe after the baby was born, they could fly out to Iowa and throw a party to celebrate both birth and matrimony.

She didn't tell Logan the truth—that despite her certainty that night, doubts had come crashing in on her since then. A part of her couldn't bear to have her extended family all there. She feared they would guess the wedding was not a union of two loving people of like minds. That they would take one look at Shani and realize the love flowed only one way. She was sure her mother would know in an instant and that the aunts and uncles would divine the truth by osmosis. So she convinced Logan that with the short notice, an intimate wedding would be best.

Sure enough, her mother sensed her daughter's misgivings the moment Shani picked her up at Sacramento International. Shani had plenty of opportunities to share her qualms—on the drive home from the airport while Rachael dozed in the backseat, in the afternoons as they sat together in the newly secured guest cottage, while they shopped for Shani's dress. But despite the pointed looks her mother gave her, Shani kept her uneasiness to herself.

Her wedding day—New Year's Day—dawned bone-chillingly cold, disappointing Shani's sister, who'd expected balmy Los Angeles temperatures during the Northern California winter. But Rachael's excitement over the wedding soon preempted her complaints about the Iowa-like weather.

An hour before the two o'clock wedding, Shani, Rachael and her mother closeted themselves in Shani's room to dress and fix their hair. Rachael's teenage effervescence as she styled Shani's hair and helped position the antique pearl-studded headpiece should have lifted Shani's spirits, but she couldn't seem to shake the sense of wrongness in the day.

Shani's mother finally shooed Rachael from the room, pleading a headache, asking her to check with Logan for some aspirin. As her sister slipped out, Shani stared at herself in the mirror, wishing she could evade the upcoming conversation.

Fussing with her hair, she pulled the veil over her face and studied her image through the wispy tulle. "It's a beautiful dress."

The close-fitting sleeves of the cream-colored raw-silk shift just brushed her wrist bone. The sweetheart neckline barely clung to her shoulders and had required a strapless bra. They'd had to alter the dress to allow for her expanding waistline, but the dress looked lovely on her nonetheless.

Her mother came up behind her and put an arm around her waist. "I thought you'd be happier on your wedding day." Despite her smile at their reflection, Shani heard the serious tone in her mother's voice.

Shani blinked back tears. "I'm just nervous."

"Uh-huh." Her mother turned her around to face her. "Talk to me, sweetheart."

Shani moved to sit on the edge of her bed. "I knew the decision was right when I made it. Now…"

Mrs. Jacoby sat beside her, took her hand. "You're not sure if you love him?"

Her eyes filled. "That's the one thing I'm sure of."

"Then what's the problem?" her mother asked gently. "You love him, he loves you…."

Shani stared down at her hands, tears dropping. Her throat was so tight, she could barely squeeze words past the constriction. "He doesn't love me, Mom."

Her mother patted her hand. "Of course he does. I've seen the way he looks at you."

Shani shook her head. "He's made it clear that love has nothing to do with our marriage. Whatever you've seen in him…"

Mrs. Jacoby tipped up Shani's chin. "You know you can stop this. Just say the word."

"I don't want to." Despite the potential for pain, she knew she couldn't turn back. "I want to find a way to make a life with him."

"And the baby."

At that reminder, joy spread inside her. "Yes. We'll have the baby."

Rachael returned then, scolding Shani for ruining her makeup with her tears. The teenager repaired the damage, then did a touch-up of her own hair. They both kissed their mother as she slipped from the room and headed for her seat downstairs.

The sound of music sifted upstairs—the opening sounds of Pachelbel. Her hand on the door, Rachael turned back to Shani. "Ready?"

Shani stood frozen, suddenly terrified, a response stuck in her throat.

Despite his determination to remain cool and detached during the last-minute prep of his wedding, Logan broke into a cold sweat with the opening notes of Pachelbel's "Canon in D Major." With the living room furniture pushed aside, a half-dozen chairs set up facing where Logan stood near the front door, he had an unimpeded view of the second-floor landing where Shani would soon appear.

"No backing out now," a voice rumbled softly in his ear.

He glanced over at his friend, Judge Jeanie Wilcox, whom he'd asked to officiate. He couldn't seem to muster an answer, so he just nodded, giving her what was likely a poor excuse for a smile.

He'd been certain over the past few weeks that Shani would, at any moment, turn to him and tell him she'd changed her mind, that her agreement had been a mistake. He'd rushed her into this marriage for exactly that reason—to give her no time to back out. Even now, he wondered if, as she started down the stairs, she would make that declaration. That she'd toss away the bouquet of orchids and baby's breath she and her mother had so laboriously picked out and lock herself in her room.

He never should have left her alone these past several days. He'd had some crazy idea that the more time she spent with him, the more likelihood there was that she'd uncover his myriad faults, find more justification to put on the brakes. It had been maddening, having her so near and not making love to her. Having tasted the treasures of her body and then holding back. But he'd been afraid of doing or saying the wrong thing. Of ruining everything.

Now he fixed his gaze on the door to her room, waiting for her to appear. For a crazy moment he wondered if she'd somehow escaped unseen, shimmying down the trellis outside her room, leaving her mother and sister behind. Anything to avoid marrying him.

Finally her sister stepped out, a small bouquet of lavender daisies clutched in her hands. She wore a dress that matched the flowers, her long hair upswept. Looking at her face, Logan could imagine Shani at that age, just as young, just as innocent. What would it have been like if he'd met her then, before he knew Arianna?

As Rachael walked along the landing and down the first step, a shadow shifted on the door to Shani's room. The Canon continued its lilting strains as the few guests seated in his living room looked expectantly up at the landing. Shani's mother, looking happy and troubled all at once. Vince and Charlotte Anzalone, beaming in expectation of what should be a joyful occasion. Mrs. Singh and her daughter, their eyes bright with good wishes. Shani's friend Julie, whose suspicious look hadn't faded from the moment she'd arrived.

If Shani had had her way, his father would be here, as well. But there was no way he was opening that can of worms.

Rachael had reached the halfway point on the stairs. That had been the signal for Shani to start her walk. Logan held himself in place by strength of will. It was all he could do to keep from going up after her.

And then his bride stepped into view.

His knees quite literally went weak at his first sight of her. The dress she'd refused to let him see fitted her perfectly, revealing and reveling in the slight curve of her ripening belly rather than hiding it. The antique veil his grandmother had worn softened Shani's beautiful face, turning it into a mystery he itched to investigate. The orchids, ivory touched with accents of lavender, trembled in her hands, but her steps down the stairs were sure.

Arianna's necklace gleamed at her throat, the unicorn pendant suspended just above the shadow between her breasts. The way the dress just barely clung to her creamy shoulders sent a shaft of desire through him as he imagined slipping it the rest of the way off as he undressed her tonight.

How the hell would he ever wait for tonight?

She arrived at his side, her gaze fixing for several long moments with his. The flush of color along her cheekbones told him she'd seen the fire in his eyes. There was an answer in that pale rose blush, the way her lips parted and her breath caught. He relaxed infinitesimally. This at least he could do right with her. He would make her body sing and send her to paradise.

She turned from him toward the judge, and the ribbon threading through her bouquet shook as she drew in a tremulous breath. Judge Wilcox's words buzzed in his mind, their sense lost. He managed to speak his part on cue, the rehearsal they'd run through the night before his saving grace. Shani's "I do" sprang without hesitation from her mouth, and in those few short minutes, the ceremony was finished.

Except for the final ritual. Not only permission, but exhortation to do what he'd ached to do again a thousand times since that December night three weeks ago. They would do it in front of a half-dozen or so people, he would have to show some self-control. But to kiss Shani again, he would accept any proviso.

Lifting the veil, fully exposing her face, he could barely breathe. He set his hands on her shoulders, his thumbs brushing bare skin, sending heat through him. His dark tuxedo suddenly felt too hot, too constricting. He wanted to strip aside the jacket, despite the audience.

Then she smiled, the gentle curve of her lips reaching deep inside him. Her hands settled on his waist. He lowered his mouth to hers, watching her eyes drift shut. He pressed against her, butterfly light, then more firmly, drinking her in.

How long they stood that way, speaking silently with their mouths, he didn't know. Quiet laughter brought him back to the room, made him aware the kiss had lasted much longer than he'd intended. He drew back to see the color on Shani's cheeks deepen and her hand raised to her face in obvious embarrassment.

He pressed a last kiss to her forehead, then, with his arm around her, faced the guests. Behind him, Judge Wilcox announced, "I'd like to introduce Mr. and Mrs. Logan Rafferty."

Applause, more laughter. They moved to the dining room, where staff from Il Paradiso had set up an Italian buffet. The expertly seasoned chicken parmesan and portobello risotto might as well have been ashes on his plate. He ate a few bites mechanically but didn't taste a thing, his gaze always on Shani. Every movement she made, every glance his way, mesmerized him.

Only dimly aware of the others in the room, he registered Shani's mother's relieved expression and the unexpected smile on her friend Julie's face. He was grateful they couldn't read the explicit, X-rated thoughts vividly displayed in his mind. All the ways he wanted to touch Shani, experience her exquisite body, played in an endless loop until he thought he'd explode from the tension.

After dinner they moved the chairs aside in the living room, allowing enough space for a first dance. The feel of Shani in his arms as they glided around the carpeted floor in a slow waltz overwhelmed his senses. Her gaze burned him clear to his soul, set every nerve ending on fire. He wanted to carry her upstairs, never mind the half-dozen or so guests they would leave behind.

But he released Shani to dance with Vince and took Mrs. Jacoby as his partner. She smiled up at him, a quiet joy lighting her face. "I'm so glad you two found each other," Shani's mother said softly.

He felt a twinge of guilt inside, knowing that this marriage wasn't the love match Mrs. Jacoby likely assumed. He cast about in his mind for an appropriate response. "We're fortunate." He winced inwardly at the pallid words.

Shani's mother regarded him with those all-too-knowing eyes. "You love each other. That's a fortune beyond price."

He had to look away, his internal tumult no doubt visible in his face. As wise as she was, couldn't she sense that the kind of love she spoke about wasn't a factor between Shani and him? Could she be baiting him, hoping for an admission of the truth? But that kind of deviousness wasn't in the straightforward Mrs. Jacoby. She must truly think he loved Shani, that she loved him.

"Make her happy," Mrs. Jacoby said, then drew back as Strauss's final notes faded.

He had a sense he'd been put to a test he hadn't quite

passed. But he had no further opportunity to speak with Shani's mother privately. He danced with Rachael, then Charlotte. Charlotte had a few bawdy suggestions for the wedding night, as if he needed further encouragement.

They cut the cake at three-thirty, Logan feeding Shani bites of zuppa inglese, stroking the creamy white frosting from her mouth with his thumb. The fever between them intensified again and he had to tamp down the urge to escort the guests from the house so he could be alone with Shani.

Thankfully, the guests began filtering out around four. First Vince and Charlotte, then Julie and Mrs. Singh. Mrs. Jacoby begged off any further visiting, pleading a return of her headache. He walked Shani's mother and her giggling younger sister to the cottage, then returned to his wife.

His wife. His sense of pride, of possessiveness, surprised him. When he'd married Arianna, he'd felt affection, respect. He'd looked forward to a good life with her. But he'd never experienced the single-minded absorption for her that he felt now for Shani.

He thought she might be in her own room, changing. But when he nudged open the unlatched door, the room was empty. Her dress lay draped over the back of the desk chair, the cream-colored pumps nearby. The light in the bathroom was off.

Anticipation tingling along his arms, up his spine, he backed from the room and headed down the hall toward his own. As he stepped inside, he heard the fall of water in his adjoining bath. The shower running. Panties and a strapless bra in a puddle of ivory panty hose just outside the bathroom door.

His heart stuttered in his chest, then slammed into hyperspeed as he stared at that untidy pile. His hands shaking, he wrestled out of the jacket, unknotted the bow tie, nearly tore the buttons from his shirt. Shucked quickly out of his pants, nearly tangling them on his shoes when he forgot to remove them first. Finally threw aside the last of his clothes.

He stepped inside the expansive bathroom, steam roiling from the open shower. Without a door or curtain to block his view, he could take in every inch of Shani's body where she stood in the middle of the shower's three jets. As he watched, she rinsed the last of the soap from her skin, then dried her eyes on a nearby towel.

His presence didn't startle her; he had the sense she'd been expecting him, waiting for him. A faint smile curved her mouth as his gaze raked her, taking in the soft swell of her breasts, the nipples taut, her belly just slightly rounded with nearly four months of pregnancy. She was glorious in her nudity, an incredible gift. Far beyond anything he could have dreamed of as perfection.

She stretched out a beckoning hand and he stepped into the shower with her. The warm spray of water hitting his flesh only added to his arousal, the first contact of his body against hers making him impossibly hard. He closed his arms around her, covering her mouth with his, his tongue immediately plunging inside.

Water sprayed them from three sides, striking his back, his sides, his arms. The wet heat stoked his fire, sensitizing him until he thought he would climax against her instead of inside where he wanted so desperately to be. She ran her hands down his sides, to his hips, his buttocks, pulling him tightly against her, moaning low in her throat.

Urgency built inside him to back her into a corner of the slick tile shower, lift her legs around his hips and thrust into her. His passion edged on the uncontrollable, a mindless and incoherent beast, frightening in its intensity. That he might hurt her sobered him, stealing some of the power from the insanity that had overtaken him, throwing him a thin lifeline of restraint.

Reaching around her, he shut off the shower, grabbing a bath sheet in the same movement. Draping it around her, he lifted her into his arms. As he carried her into the bedroom, her mouth sipped at his chest, licking the moisture from his skin, driving him into madness again.

He set her on her feet to pull back the covers. She waited until he'd turned toward her to slowly lower the towel, taunting him with her beauty.

He stopped her before she could move toward the bed, dropping to his knees before her. She was a goddess to be worshipped, and he intended to give her her due. He buried his mouth in the curls between her legs, tugging apart her folds with his thumbs. She sucked in a breath with the first touch of his tongue, her fingers digging into his shoulders.

With a hand spread at the small of her back to support her, he continued to taste her as his other hand moved lazily along her inner thigh. He trailed his fingers nearly to the juncture, then away, in rhythm with the stroking of his tongue, teasing her with each skimming touch. Her body shook as if she could barely stay upright and he tightened his hold on her, continuing his sensual assault.

Her fingers gripped so hard, he knew she would leave her mark on him. He could feel her climax lapping at her, the first trembling wave. He plunged his fingers inside her slick opening, felt her moan vibrate along his skin. Her body clutched at him, again and again, closing around his fingers deep inside her body.

He kept his hold on her as he rose to his feet, could feel the lassitude in her body, the aftereffects of pleasure still strumming along her skin. Urging her to the bed, he parted her legs and settled between them. Her eyes opened languidly and she reached for him, pulling him inside her.

There wasn't a chance in hell he would last long. From her urgent cries, he knew she was right with him, didn't want him holding back. Her legs locked around his hips, pushing him in deeper, calling out his name as she peaked. He exploded, his body hurled into ecstasy, blown into a universe of sensation. Shani his only anchor, his climax flung him into a perfect light, beyond himself, beyond reality.

As sanity returned, his breathing still unsteady and difficult, he became aware of his body, heavy on hers. He tried to edge away, off her, but she held him in place, her strength surprising. He eased up on his elbows to give her some relief, but she didn't let go for several minutes.

Finally she sighed, her arms going lax. He slid to her side, gathering her close to him. His gold band snagged on the sheets and a thrill shot through him. She was his wife. He could make love to her every night if he wanted to. Her lovely face would be the last thing he saw before he closed his eyes to sleep, the first thing he saw in the morning.

Her hair, still damp, tickled his chest as he nestled her head against him. "Are you sure you don't want a honeymoon?" he asked her.

She stiffened slightly, then relaxed so quickly, he wondered if he'd imagined it. "I told you, I signed up for that winter-break class."

"Drop it. Take it later."

"I need it to graduate in May."

He stroked her cheek with his fingers. "Why not wait until next semester to graduate, give yourself more time?"

She lay silent for so long, he half wondered if she'd fallen asleep. When she spoke, the trembling in her voice set off an ache inside him.

"You've changed everything else in my life, Logan. Please don't change this."

He felt moisture under his thumb where he stroked her face, and when he angled himself up, he saw her tears. "Shani."

She turned her back to him, edging just slightly out of reach. The ache inside him sharpened. How many times had he said the wrong thing to Arianna and sent her into silent tears?

He scrambled for a way to make things right. "Shani," he whispered, praying she'd look at him.

She drew in a breath, then dropped a kiss in the palm of his hand. "It's just been a long day." She faced him again. "Too much to take in all at once."

She pressed closer to him, her skin warm and silky against his. Far sooner than he would have expected, he was ready for her, his erection pressing against her belly.

"You make me crazy," he murmured in her ear.

"No more than you make me." Her hand drifted down his side.

They started the dance again, this time more slowly. But with each touch, each kiss bringing them both closer to the precipice, Logan couldn't quite shake the memory of Shani's silent tears.

Chapter Fourteen

January passed quickly, Shani so caught up in her inter-session class, her hours at work and the daily ups and downs of pregnancy, she barely had a moment to stop and think about the life-changing event she'd undergone. To anyone on the outside—her coworkers, her friends at school, even Mrs. Singh—there was nothing remarkable about her marriage to Logan. She got some good-natured ribbing from some of the staff at MiniSport, but by the time it became generally known that she'd married the CEO of the company, they also knew the back story—she'd been a longtime friend of Arianna and had known Logan for years. So her coworkers accepted it, or at least kept their personal opinions to themselves.

She moved into Logan's room on her wedding night. After the first two weeks she lost count of the number of times they made love. Each encounter only drove Logan deeper into her heart, added power to the love she felt for him. When she reached her peak during their lovemaking, she could all but feel that love pour from her in a tidal wave of emotion. It was all she could do to keep silent, to hold back the words she ached to speak aloud.

After that first night she refused to let tears fall when uncertainty lapped at her. With a single exception, Logan gave her everything any woman could want. He was attentive, spending as much of his free time with her as he could. When he had to work late, he'd call, sometimes more than once to update her. He surprised her with gifts—a thriller novel she mentioned in passing, a beautiful cashmere sweater in deep coral he saw in a hotel gift shop on a business trip, flowers out of the blue on a Thursday afternoon. And there was the baby—thanks to the paperwork Logan's attorney had filed, the child she bore was hers. She was the baby's legal mother, not just a gestational carrier.

She told herself it was enough. Most of the time she even believed it. It was only late at night, when she couldn't sleep and she lay listening to Logan's steady breathing beside her, that she doubted. That she couldn't put aside her awareness of that hole in her life, the absence of love from the man she loved so deeply.

In those dark moments, only one thought kept the tears at bay—that he would learn to love her. That after time, maybe with the birth of his child, he would open up his heart to her. That he would realize she was as precious to him as he had become to her.

On the day of her five-month checkup during the first week of February, Logan stood with her in the examination room, staring at the ultrasound image, rapt. The 3-D image delineated the baby's face, hands and fingers. Arms, legs, and…

"He's a boy," Logan said, his gaze fixed on the image.

Dr. Mills, the ob-gyn, grinned. "That he is. And everything looks great, Dad."

Shani couldn't hold back the sudden rush of emotion. *Another son.* Despite her best efforts, tears sprang into her eyes.

She tried to turn her head away to keep Logan from seeing, but he spotted the wet trail on her cheek. He laced his fingers into hers, squeezing. Then he leaned over to press a kiss to her cheek. "Another son," he whispered, too softly for the doctor to hear.

That he understood her tears, that he'd echoed her thought exactly, nearly undid her. She dragged in several deep breaths to ease the pain locked in her heart, all the while clutching Logan's hand.

When Dr. Mills left the room, Logan helped her clean the gel from her belly, then waited while she dressed. "Do you have time for lunch?" he asked.

"Sure," she said, her throat still raw from emotion.

He took her to the crepe restaurant, but with the lunchtime crowd, the wait was nearly thirty minutes. The hostess gestured toward the patio. "I can seat you right away if you don't mind eating outdoors. There's a gas heater. It'll keep you warm."

Still feeling on the edge of falling apart, Shani glanced out at the empty patio. "Let's eat outside." She'd just as soon not have an audience if she couldn't hold back her tears.

As they stepped outside, Shani spotted a dark green Nissan pulling out of the parking lot. A jolt of fear went through her. In the months since she'd last seen the car, she'd let herself believe its appearances were coincidental. Seeing it now, with her emotions already in an uproar, she was flooded with doubt and unease.

"What is it?" Logan asked as they were seated by the heater.

The car had pulled up the street and out of sight. Shani shook off her anxiety. "It's nothing. Just feeling a little unsteady."

Logan took a cursory look at his menu before setting it aside. "I could skip the conference this weekend."

He'd told her the week before about his commitment to speak at a conference in Phoenix. "There's no need," Shani told him. "I'll be fine."

He reached across the table to take her hand. "Will you?"

She could see the seriousness of his expression, the worry in his blue eyes. "Why wouldn't I be?"

His thumb traced across the backs of her fingers. "You've seemed sad lately."

Apparently she didn't hide her feelings as well as she'd thought. "Not sad, so much as…emotional."

His gaze remained steady on her face. "Arianna would never tell me. When she felt sad or upset. I was constantly guessing, never sure what I was supposed to do to fix it."

"Sometimes it's not up to you to fix," Shani said gently. "Sometimes the person feeling that way has to come to terms with it themselves."

His focus dropped to the table. "Except it seemed I was always the one who'd caused the problem in the first place."

A question that had been lurking in the back of her mind sprang from her lips before she could stop herself. "Did you love her?"

The moment she'd let herself speak the words out loud, the instant she saw the anger, guilt and sorrow flash across his face, she wanted to rewind the past few seconds. "I'm sorry," she said. "That was out of line."

He let go of her hand. "What did the diary say?"

"I thought you didn't want to know."

"I don't." Knuckles tightening as he lifted his glass, he took a sip of ice water. "But I'm sure Arianna made it clear I never measured up. Or ever gave her what she really wanted."

His gaze flickered in her direction before dropping again. "I thought I loved her. I wanted to." He slid the glass side to side on the white tablecloth. "But based on experience, I never quite achieved that goal."

"I think you achieved more than you know," Shani said. "Yes, she wrote about you in her diary…of course she did. But as time went on, she began to realize her sadness was inside her and not your doing. In time, if she hadn't died—"

"Nothing would have changed."

"It might have."

"I couldn't be who she wanted." He stared at her. "If you're looking for the same thing from me as Arianna was, I think you'll be just as disappointed."

"So far nothing you've done has disappointed me."

"You shouldn't lie, Shani," he said, his tone bitter. "You don't do it well."

The joy she'd seen in Logan when he watched his son on the ultrasound seemed to have vanished, chased by ghosts of guilt and recrimination. When the waitress came to take their order, Shani chose something at random from the menu. She leaned as close as she could to the heater as they waited for their food, but although the February day wasn't particularly chilly, she couldn't seem to get warm.

She assumed they'd finish the meal in silence, that Logan was done with revisiting the past. But as Shani picked at her crepe, Logan spoke, pain in the soft rumbling of his voice.

"I should have stopped her that night. Should have kept her from driving away."

"It was an accident, Logan. Not your fault."

He dipped his head in acknowledgment. "We argued right before she left. Over something stupid. I wanted to stay home for dinner, she wanted to go out. I don't even know why I made such a federal case out of it. I'd had a bad day at work, was beat."

His jaw worked. "I should have stopped her when she ran out of the house. Should have kept her from that car. But I was too full of my own damned pride."

"You couldn't have known what would happen."

"But she was upset. She was crying. Not thinking straight."

He picked up his fork, set it down again, stared at his food growing cold on his plate. "I thought she'd just drive around the neighborhood, then come home. Or go out to eat alone. Instead, she went up Highway 50. On her way to Tahoe, I guess—she had a friend up there. She hit the curve past Horsetail Falls going at least fifty…"

Well over the speed limit, and the drop-off was too steep for survival. When Arianna's sister had called Shani, making her way down the contact list on Arianna's cell, that image of her friend going over the cliff had been horrifying. Shani hadn't yet brought herself to drive that part of Highway 50 in the year and a half since Arianna's death.

Logan seemed as distant as that stretch of road a hundred miles away and just as desolate as the wilderness surrounding Horsetail Falls. Shani couldn't bear to see him lost in that dark place. She moved her chair next to him, put her arms around him.

He stiffened, seemed ready to pull back. Then he

relaxed into her embrace, burying his face in her hair. She was grateful for the solitude of the patio, glad for the chance to give something to Logan he so seldom seemed willing to accept—comfort.

Then she felt the brush of a miracle and a giddy joy filled her. "The baby just moved," she whispered, as if their son could hear.

Logan's hand went immediately to her belly. "Where?"

She laughed and covered his hand with hers. "It's probably too early for you to feel. It feels almost like gas, like a tickling inside."

Still, he kept his hand against her, his other arm wrapped around her shoulders. "Arianna never kept her pregnancy long enough for me to feel the baby move."

"I know."

He stroked her rounded abdomen, his breath curling in her ear as he said softly, "Thank you, Shani."

If she let her imagination run wild, she could hear "I love you" in his whispered words. But that kind of fantasy would only be courting heartbreak. Instead, she'd savor this moment of happiness, build on it what she could, repressing her longings for the impossible.

This wasn't Logan's first business trip in the six weeks since they'd married, but the first one encompassing the weekend. During the week, Shani had so much to keep her busy, she had less time to dwell on missing Logan, and was tired enough at night she'd fall asleep quickly.

After a long workday and an hour on the phone with Logan, she slept well enough on Friday night. On Saturday, she took a good, long walk around the neighborhood, shadowed by Patrick Cade's man, then lay down for a nap. She slept longer than she'd intended, waking with her lower back sore from the unaccustomed exercise.

She discovered after her nap that she'd missed Logan's phone call. She couldn't reach him all afternoon, his cell no doubt switched off during his presentation at the conference. They weren't able to touch base until seven, and he kept his call short because she'd just sat down to dinner. She tried him again at nine, but yawned her way through their conversation, exhaustion weighing on her. Yet when she climbed into bed, her aching back and too much sleep in the afternoon kept her wakeful until past two.

She woke the next morning feeling tired and cranky, the ache in her back exacerbated from sleeping awkwardly. She had little appetite for the breakfast Mrs. Singh fixed for her, the housekeeper's usually delicious blueberry muffins unappealing. At eleven-thirty, she dozed off at the desk in the master bedroom as she struggled to craft an essay for her employment law class.

Shutting the laptop, she stumbled to the bed and dropped into it, asleep almost instantly. She had strange, disjointed dreams and struggled to awareness several times before she could finally wake herself.

She lay there, muzzy and disoriented, squinting at the clock. The time shocked her—nearly one. She couldn't believe she'd slept so long. She felt even more out of sorts than before her nap, unhappy that Logan wasn't expected home for another three hours.

She pushed herself vertical, then dropped her feet to the floor. Her lower back throbbed in uneasy warning. As she pushed to her feet, excruciating pain stabbed the base of her spine. At the same moment, she felt wetness between her legs.

"No," she moaned.

The pain intensified, doubling her over. She forced herself to the bedroom door, her ears roaring from the agony. Every muscle trembling, Shani reached the railing of the landing and leaned over it.

Please, God, let Mrs. Singh be nearby. She vaguely remembered the housekeeper mentioning she had to do the week's marketing today. Shani prayed she hadn't left yet.

"Mrs. Singh!" she called downstairs as loudly as she could. No answer. She yelled again, gasping as another shaft of agony shot down her leg.

Trying to breathe through the pain, she remembered the phone back in the bedroom. She turned to call 911 herself, but another lance of pain stole the strength from her legs. She sank to the floor, tears filling her eyes.

She dragged in breath after breath, willing herself to stand again. She felt another trickle of wetness, and despair filled her.

"Mrs. Singh!" she screamed out, but the silent house told Shani the housekeeper was gone. Tears flooded her cheeks as she gripped the baluster. She had to get herself into the bedroom, to a phone.

The rattle of a door lock caught her attention and her heart lifted in sudden relief. "Mrs. Singh?"

"Shani?" Logan's voice called out.

"Upstairs! Logan, I need you."

Logan took off at a dead run at Shani's terrifying plea, racing from the kitchen, through the living room, up the stairs three at a time. Seeing her crumpled by the railing, his heart felt as if it would explode in his chest. Without conscious thought, he scooped her up and hurried back downstairs with her in his arms.

"You weren't getting home until four," she said, her voice ragged.

"Got on an earlier flight." He pushed the garage door open and shouldered through. "I had to get home."

He set her gently in the Mercedes, then hit the garage door opener before running around to the driver's side. The garage door had barely cleared the roof of the car before he backed out, the screeching of tires attracting the attention of Patrick Cade's man, who'd just emerged from around the side of the house. Logan shouted out to the security guard, "Taking Shani to the hospital," before gunning down the drive and out the gate.

Each trip he'd taken away from Shani had been harder to bear, each one lonelier than the last. At the conference, he'd been preoccupied with Shani nearly every waking moment, stumbling more than once during his well-rehearsed workshop on innovation and marketing. When he'd phoned yesterday during her nap, Mrs. Singh had offered to wake Shani, but he knew she needed her rest. They played telephone tag the rest of the afternoon, and when they finally connected, their interaction was abbreviated and unsatisfying.

Thank God he'd given in to his weakness and decided to return early. He'd given a keynote speech at an early-morning breakfast meeting and had promised to attend the luncheon before heading home. But once he'd completed his speech, he couldn't stand to spend another moment in Phoenix. He called the airline to reschedule his flight and was on his way to Sky Harbor twenty minutes later.

He glanced over at Shani, his stomach constricting at her pale face. "What's going on?"

"It hurts," she said faintly. "My back. Down the back of my leg. And I felt something wet on my panties."

His mind immediately flew to the worst option. "Blood?"

"I don't know. I never got a chance to check. It hurt too much."

An icy chill shot down his spine. "Are you cramping?" That was how it had started with Arianna. Cramping, then bleeding, then...

"Sharper pain," Shani said.

Thank God the hospital was only ten miles away in Folsom. No freeway route to get there, though, so it would take nearly twenty minutes, even pushing the speed limit along Auburn-Folsom Road. At every stoplight, he wanted to slam his fist into the horn to move the other cars out of the way.

At Mercy Hospital, he arrowed into the first empty space he could find, then hurried around to Shani. He carried her in to the emergency entrance, praying for a miracle, struggling to hold hopelessness at bay.

Spotting a wheelchair as he stepped inside, he gently set Shani down in it, then hurried over to one of the admitting clerks. "My wife is five months pregnant," he told the middle-aged woman behind the counter. "She's in pain. I think she might be..."

He couldn't say the word *miscarrying* out loud, but the clerk understood. "Let me call OB." She picked up the phone and carried on a rapid-fire conversation.

While they waited for the nurse, Logan started the paperwork process with the admitting clerk. He hadn't quite finished when the nurse arrived, but the clerk waved him off to accompany Shani.

He helped Shani undress, letting her clutch his hand when the pain was particularly bad. After getting Shani settled on the bed in her blue gown, the nurse strapped a fetal monitor around Shani's waist. As they waited for the doctor, Shani looked so small, so frightened, a hole opened in Logan's chest seeing her that way.

"I need to tell you something." She glanced up at him, her expression grave. "If I lose the baby—"

"Don't say it." Saying it out loud might make it real.

"But if I do…" She took in a long breath. "There's no reason for us to be married anymore."

The air left his lungs; he couldn't muster a response. Was the baby the only reason Shani stayed with him? Had he fooled himself into thinking there was more to their union than the child she carried? How could he blame her, when he couldn't give her the one thing she'd asked for, valued above all else?

Before they could continue the discussion, the doctor entered. "Mr. and Mrs. Rafferty, I'm Dr. Jack Hanford."

The doctor checked the readout on the fetal monitor. "No contractions. The baby's heartbeat seems regular." He pulled on a pair of latex gloves and positioned Shani's legs up in stirrups.

The doctor scooted his stool over to examine Shani. "The cervix is still in good shape. No effacement. Let's check those vaginal secretions."

The man obtained a sample, then smeared a swab onto a glass slide. "Have to check this under the scope."

After he left the room, Logan bent to press a kiss to Shani's forehead. "You're going to be fine," he murmured in her ear.

A few moments later, Dr. Hanford returned. "Not amniotic fluid. Just normal vaginal discharge. That can get a little heavier with pregnancy."

Shani's hand tightened around Logan's fingers. "What about the pain?"

"Any discomfort in the abdominal area?"

Shani shifted on the bed, her discomfort clear. "No. Just my lower back and down the back of my leg."

Dr. Hanford pulled off his gloves. "Your pain is likely sciatica. Still not much fun, but not labor. Sciatica's usually more of a problem later in pregnancy."

Logan was afraid to believe the good news. "She's not miscarrying?"

He shook his head. "Just to be safe, we'll do an ultrasound to make sure the fluid level around the baby is normal. Assuming everything continues to check out, we'll send you home with some Vicodin for the pain."

"Is that safe for the baby?" Shani asked.

"Narcotics are actually a little safer than anti-inflammatories at this stage of the game."

With that pronouncement, Dr. Hanford strode from the room. Logan carefully gathered his wife in his arms, soaking up her tears as she cried quietly. When he straightened, his hand still linked in hers, she smiled up at him, her eyes red but her expression joyful.

"It still hurts like the dickens," she told him, the angles of her face sharp from the pain. "But I don't even care. Just the thought that we might have lost him…"

He smoothed her hair back, wishing he could draw the hurt from her body into his own. As grateful as he was that the baby was fine, that the threat of miscarriage had been a false alarm, he realized he had more reason than the baby's health to rejoice.

Shani wouldn't be leaving him.

Chapter Fifteen

The first Saturday in spring, Mrs. Singh went into a frenzy of cleaning, going through the main house like a sanitation tornado. While under strict orders from Logan to avoid any heavy lifting, Shani worked alongside the housekeeper, dusting as Mrs. Singh vacuumed, or scrubbing the windows she could reach without climbing on a ladder.

Mrs. Singh appreciated the company and Shani enjoyed the work. She needed the break from the mental exercise of term papers and senior thesis, needed something that didn't take any more brain power than what was required to squirt window cleaner on a pane of glass.

Finished with the guest room Shani had once used and all the first-floor rooms, they'd made their way upstairs into the master bedroom. In preparation for dusting the massive mahogany dresser, Shani had shifted all the lightweight odds and ends from it to the desk Logan had moved from the guest room for her. With furniture polish on a soft rag, she buffed the top of the dresser as Mrs. Singh worked in the bathroom.

Just as Shani gave a last swipe of her cloth on the dresser, the housekeeper exited the master bath with her bucket of cleaning supplies. She held out a paperback book to Shani. "I found this in the vanity, in a bottom drawer. Arianna must have left it there."

A romance novel, Shani saw from the cover. Arianna had loved them, their hopeful messages, their happy endings.

Shani opened it to where a bookmark had been tucked inside. "Looks like this is as far as she got in the book." Sadness tightened Shani's throat at the reminder of an unfinished life.

The slip of paper fluttered from the book to the floor. As Shani retrieved it, she noticed an e-mail address written on it, in Arianna's flowing script. Shani didn't recognize the address. She set the paper and the book on the nightstand.

Mrs. Singh rolled in the vacuum from the hall, then leaned on the handle as Shani replaced the items on the dresser. "I'm glad things are working out well for you and Mr. Rafferty," she said as she played out the cord for the vacuum. "That man deserves his happiness."

"Have you worked for Mr. Rafferty a long time?" Shani asked as she carefully positioned Arianna's glass paperweight on Logan's side of the dresser.

"Since before he married the first Mrs. Rafferty. A friend of my mother's worked for his father and recommended me."

Mrs. Singh started the vacuum, the noise precluding conversation for the moment. Nevertheless, the questions tumbled in Shani's mind.

How much might that friend have told Mrs. Singh about Logan's childhood? What insight could the housekeeper give Shani about her husband to better understand him?

In the nearly three months since their marriage, as her love for Logan grew, becoming almost too painful to keep inside, her longing to discover a way inside his heart had become a near obsession. She'd reread the diary, pored over each page where Logan was mentioned, scrutinizing each word for a clue. She'd gone back to the cottage, scouring the closet and dresser drawers, hoping to find the missing diary pages that might provide enlightenment.

She still felt as in the dark about Logan as she had when she'd first reentered his life last summer. How could a man who could seem so caring be at the same time so aloof? His solicitousness after their emergency room scare had been so comforting. The three days she lay bedridden from the sciatica he'd jumped to fulfill her every need, and after the doctor gave her the all clear, his tenderness when they made love touched her to her very core. But even still, there was always a barrier between them, a wall she could never quite penetrate.

Mrs. Singh shut off the vacuum and started wrapping the cord. Logan would be up here soon to turn the mattress. If Shani intended to interrogate Mrs. Singh, she'd better do it quickly.

She set the polishing cloth down on the desk. "Do you know anything about him when he was younger?"

Mrs. Singh rolled the vacuum over by the door. "Help me strip the bed so it's ready for Mr. Rafferty."

Working opposite the housekeeper, Shani peeled away the comforter, then the other bedding. After they set the pillows on the side chairs and pulled off the fitted sheet and mattress pad, Mrs. Singh sat on the edge of the bed, gesturing to Shani to sit beside her.

"My mother's friend worked there the first few years after Mr. Rafferty's mother died. She would tell my mother stories…" Mrs. Singh shook her head. "At the time, I was a new wife with my firstborn on the way, just like you."

Mrs. Singh didn't know about Shani's first son, but Shani kept her twinge of pain and its cause to herself. "What stories?"

"This friend, Mrs. Patel, worked as housekeeper and nanny. Sometimes, she would return from her days off to find no one there watching the child. Mr. Rafferty's father would leave him there alone."

Meeting Mrs. Singh's dark gaze, Shani could see the housekeeper's horror matched her own. "But he was only seven when his mother died."

Mrs. Singh nodded. "One day she arrived to discover the boy had fallen from a tree in the backyard and broken his arm. A neighbor heard him crying and took him to the doctor. It took hours to find his father."

Shani couldn't hold back tears of empathy for that poor scared boy. Mrs. Singh took her hand and patted it. "There were other stories."

"I don't have to hear them." What Mrs. Singh had revealed had been enough to clarify the path Logan had taken to become the man he was today. That he could be kind at all to her, that bitterness hadn't eaten him up inside, was a miracle.

At the sound of the front door slamming and footsteps up the stairs, Shani and Mrs. Singh both jumped to their feet, then looked at each other. They laughed like guilty children.

Logan entered, Patrick Cade at his heels. The

owner of the security firm had arrived this morning, substituting for one of his employees so the woman could celebrate her daughter's first birthday. He and Logan had been outside all morning testing the security system.

Patrick was at least a couple of inches taller than Logan's six foot two, even broader in the shoulders, his close-cropped hair dark blond and his piercing eyes green. Polite and soft-spoken, he was even more taciturn than Logan, likely with just as many secrets.

"I roped Patrick into giving me a hand with that mattress," Logan said.

Patrick nodded at Shani and Mrs. Singh as the two women backed away to give the men room. They muscled the king-size mattress up off the box springs as if it was featherlight, rotating it and flipping it to Mrs. Singh's satisfaction.

"Any other heavy work you need done before we go back outside?" Logan asked.

"I think that's it," Shani said.

Before they headed out, Logan surprised her, pulling her in his arms for a very thorough kiss. When he stepped away, Shani saw Mrs. Singh occupying herself with the mattress pad, but Patrick had his gaze fixed on them in frank observation, a faint smile on his face, one brow raised.

Then the men were gone. Heat lingered in Shani's face, but she felt too darn happy to be embarrassed.

Mrs. Singh came around the bed and gave her a hug. "It's good that he's found someone to love again."

Shani didn't correct her, wanting to hold the golden moment to herself. Wanting to believe that maybe Mrs. Singh spoke the truth.

They quickly made up the bed, then moved on to the

other rooms on the second floor, another guest room and bath and a rarely used study. The time went quickly as they discussed what they'd do to convert the second guest room into a nursery—replace the floral wallpaper with an airplane print, exchange the dark wood dresser for something lighter to match the crib Shani had picked out. They'd have to move out the desk to make room for a changing table.

Shani had decided to leave the twin bed in the room so she could sleep in here when the baby was still small if he was having a bad night. Of course, Logan would likely squeeze in that bed with her, so it might be best to move the double bed in here.

The ringing of the phone pulled Shani from her musing. There wasn't an extension in the guest room, so she had to run back to the master bedroom to answer it.

"Hello," she gasped out when she grabbed up the phone.

There was a pause, then a vaguely familiar male voice with a trace of an Irish accent asked, "Mrs. Singh?"

"This is Mrs. Rafferty," Shani told the man.

Another pause, then a soft chuckle. "So, he married you."

A prickle of caution crawled up Shani's spine. "Who is this?"

"This would be Logan's father, Colin. I don't imagine he's told you about me."

"Not much." *But I've heard plenty,* Shani thought.

"How's the little bairn?"

She wasn't about to tell him about the baby. "What do you want?" She winced inwardly at her rude tone, but Mrs. Singh's stories were still fresh in her mind.

"I'd like to speak to my son, Mrs. Rafferty." He gasped out the last few syllables, then she heard the muffled sounds of coughing. "If you'll put him on," he added more raggedly.

Shani wanted to tell him Logan was out, that he'd have to call back. But she couldn't quite voice the lie.

"I'll get him," she said, then hurried from the bedroom.

She found Logan and Patrick on the front porch, deep in conversation. Logan must have seen something in her face, because he moved immediately toward her. "What is it?"

She held out the phone. "It's your father."

His expression darkened as he took the phone. "What do you want?" he barked out. A glance at Shani and Patrick, then he strode down the porch steps and along the gravel walkway.

Feeling an involuntary need to protect her baby, Shani locked her fingers across her belly. Patrick scrutinized her, his gaze intense. "The baby's doing well?" he asked.

The personal question surprised her. "We got a glowing report at the six-month checkup."

Pain flickered in those green eyes as he looked off across the estate's rolling verdant lawn. "Keep yourself safe."

With that cryptic comment, he descended the stairs and started toward the front gate. As she watched, he walked along the high stucco wall, beginning his rounds of the property.

Logan returned, his expression grim. "I have to leave. Probably be gone overnight."

Shani rubbed her stomach, doing her best to relax and send soothing thoughts to her son. "What is it?"

"My father's in the hospital." He let out a heavy gust of air. "He's just been diagnosed with liver cancer."

"Oh, Logan, I'm sorry." She wrapped her arms around him. He embraced her, as well.

"I shouldn't care," he murmured into her ear.

"Mrs. Singh told me…"

"About what a prize father he was?" Anger edged his tone. "Why the hell should I go to him?"

"For you, Logan, not for him. Say whatever you need to say while he's alive. I wish I had the chance to do that with my own father."

She could feel his nod. "I might end up staying over-night. Patrick will be here, or one of his men."

He kissed her then, so tenderly a knot tightened in her chest. In that moment, she realized she couldn't let him go without revealing what was in her heart.

She drew back, tipped her head back to meet his gaze. "I've tried to keep this to myself…" She couldn't hold back a smile. "I can't anymore, Logan. I love you. With every ounce of my being."

His gaze on hers didn't falter, but she couldn't read the message in his eyes. He bent to kiss her again, his mouth lingering on hers for a long time.

They went inside, Logan heading upstairs to pack an overnight bag. Back downstairs, he scooped up his car keys.

"I'll call you when I know more," he said. One last kiss, then he left.

Shani puzzled over his reaction to her admission. He didn't deny or reject her love, didn't react with anger as she thought he might. But what he did feel inside behind the barrier he put up between them was a total mystery to Shani.

Of course, he had to be preoccupied with his father's illness, with the prospect of seeing the man. When Logan returned, hopefully some of his old history with his father would be put to bed, and he would be in a better frame of mind to talk. And talk they would; she would insist on it.

* * *

It was nearly six by the time Logan reached the Alameda County Medical Center in Oakland, where his father had been admitted. As it was a hospital where the indigent and uninsured could get medical care, Colin Rafferty's presence here meant his father had run through the money Logan had given him last year.

He found his father in a room with three other patients, closest to the window, the last one in a row of beds. From the door where Logan lingered, his father looked sunken and pale, much smaller than his six-foot-plus height. His hair had thinned, gray crowding out the dark strands. Logan hadn't laid eyes on the man since Arianna's funeral a year and a half ago. He looked decades older.

Logan stepped aside for the nurse entering the room and his father turned. He smiled, the grin not so broad as Logan remembered. Logan walked toward him, feeling much like the little boy who for years had so desperately tried to please his father.

"Come to watch me die?" Colin said.

Logan tamped down his knee-jerk anger, keeping his voice even. "You asked me here."

"I guess I did." He plucked at the sheet, setting into motion the tube running from the back of his hand. His skin looked yellowed and paper-thin. "I passed out. On the damn street. They brought me here."

"How long have you known about the cancer?" Logan asked.

His father shrugged. "A month. Been feeling lousy for longer than that."

Logan remembered how his father had sounded last November when he'd called. No doubt there'd been something wrong even then. When his father didn't call again in the intervening four months, Logan had been relieved. It had never crossed his mind to wonder if his father was okay.

Guilt gnawed at him. "How much longer…?"

"You don't care," Colin snapped. "Why even ask?"

Except he did care, damn it all to hell. Despite the pain his father had caused him. Even though Colin Rafferty had abandoned him in more ways and more times than he could count.

With a sudden burst of insight, Logan realized why it mattered—because of Shani. Because she'd opened his heart to compassion, to empathy. Because if she was here, she would pour out her kindness, her graciousness, over this pitiless old man and make him just a little bit better inside.

What would it cost him to make peace with his father? Certainly not pride; Logan didn't give a damn about that. Maybe by treating his father the way Logan would have liked to be treated all these years, he would be able to transfer to his own son something better than his father had given him.

"How long are they giving you, Dad?" Logan asked again.

His father's eyes flickered to Logan's face. "Not long. Few weeks. Maybe less."

Logan let that reality settle in on him. He pulled over a chair and lowered himself in it beside the bed. "I don't know if it's in me to forgive you, if that's what you're looking for."

His father stared down at his hands, frail and lax in his lap. His Adam's apple worked as he swallowed, emphasizing the gauntness of his throat.

When he finally looked up at Logan, despair had hollowed out Colin Rafferty's eyes. "I just don't want to die alone," he whispered.

The impact of those simple words wiped away Logan's bitterness. Nothing in his father had changed—he was still a man who had inflicted far too much hurt on too many people. But Logan realized he could step back from the personal debt his father owed and simply treat him as a dying man who deserved some dignity in his last days.

Because Colin Rafferty had no one. His wife was thirty years dead, his string of women gone, as well. He'd estranged his only son.

But Logan...he had everything. Shani and a beautiful son on the way. A successful business. He could at least give his father some of his time.

"When you're stable, I'll have you moved closer to me," Logan said. "Put you in hospice care."

"Can I meet that wife of yours?" Colin asked eagerly. "That grandson of mine?"

"Sure," Logan said, although he doubted his father would last long enough to see the next generation arrive.

They sat quietly after that, Logan imagining Shani beside him, holding his hand, supporting him. Loving him.

As he loved her.

Chapter Sixteen

Shani was already in bed, curled up with a mystery, when Logan called to update her about his father. He'd be staying overnight, then tomorrow would have his father transported to a hospice-care facility in Sacramento.

"I probably won't be home until late afternoon," Logan told her. "I'd like to take you out to dinner. Talk about something."

"I'll be here." She wished she could reach through the phone and touch him. "I've got to get back to the homework I put off today."

"Shani…" he said softly, with a quiet peace that surprised her.

Something of tremendous magnitude shimmered between them, as if it had traveled along the phone lines from him to her. "Yes?"

He sighed. "Tomorrow. See you then."

They said their goodbyes and Shani set aside the

phone, thoroughly unsatisfied with how the conversation had ended. She was certain the wait until Logan's return would drag on forever.

She slept well, despite the anticipation, then spent all morning and a good portion of the afternoon plowing through the two essays due before spring break and looking over the comments her adviser had made on her senior thesis. Logan called twice, once in the morning, again just after two. The warmth in his tone tantalized her, teased her curiosity. The call left her smiling, aching for Logan to be home.

The phone rang an hour later, waking Shani from a nap. By the time she snatched up the receiver, the answering machine had picked up. She could hear the echo of the machine recording her sleepy hello.

She didn't recognize the tenor voice. "Mrs. Rafferty?" the man said.

"Yes?"

"You don't know me, but I'm calling about your friend."

"My friend…you mean Julie?"

"Yes, yes. Julie. I'm afraid I have some bad news. There was an accident."

Shani's heart thundered into overdrive. "Is she all right? Where is she?"

"It's bad, Mrs. Rafferty. She's on her way to the hospital. I have an address."

He rattled off numbers and a street name in Auburn, about fifteen miles northeast of Granite Bay. Shani fumbled for a small pad of paper on the nightstand, in her haste knocking the scrap Arianna had used for her bookmark to the floor. She scribbled the address on the pad and ripped off the top sheet.

"Turn right on Bell Road," the man said. "It's a shortcut to the hospital."

"I'll be there in twenty minutes," she told the man, then hung up.

Her fingers trembling, she punched out Logan's cell number. Voice mail cut in immediately; he must have turned his phone off while he was in the hospital. She left a hurried message, then hung up.

Mrs. Singh was in Fairfield visiting her grandchildren. Patrick Cade's man was no doubt somewhere on the premises, although Shani had no idea where. She couldn't waste time looking for the man. She'd just leave a note.

Grabbing the pad again, Shani wrote hurriedly, *Emergency—Julie in hospital, Auburn.* She dropped the pad in the middle of the bed, grabbed her purse and ran for the door. As she waited for the gate to roll open and allow her to drive through, she saw Cade's man beside the house. She waved as she left the estate.

It took Logan longer than he'd anticipated to get his father settled in a private room. There was a pile of paperwork, including a power-of-attorney form and an advance-health-care directive that needed notarizing. His father was exhausted by the time he was safely in his new room and wanted Logan to spend just a few more minutes with him.

On his way to his car, Logan pulled out his phone and switched it on to call Shani. She didn't pick up at home, nor did she answer her cell. Worried, he called the cell number Patrick used for his security staff and reached the man on duty patrolling the estate.

"Your wife left a few minutes ago, Mr. Rafferty," the man said.

"Do you know where she went?" Logan asked.

"She didn't say."

Logan hung up, worry eating at him. Shani was free to go out any time she wanted. She probably needed a break from her work. She'd be back to go out to dinner with him. He'd have his chance then to tell her what he'd been holding inside since yesterday—that he loved her.

As he pulled up to the house, he saw Mrs. Singh outside the guest cottage. Spotting him, she waved him over. Leaving the car in the drive, Logan covered the distance to the cottage on foot.

"I thought you were visiting your grandchildren today," Logan said.

"They were both sick and cranky. I left so my daughter could get them into bed." She gestured inside the cottage. "Could you help me turn another mattress?"

They went inside where Mrs. Singh had piled the bedding on the living room floor. In the bedroom, Logan hefted the double mattress from the box springs, holding it up on one edge as he waited for Mrs. Singh's direction.

"What's that?" she asked, pointing to a stack of papers centered on the box springs.

Arianna's flowing script covered the top sheet. From the size and color of the pages, they looked as if they could have come from her diary.

"Grab them. I'll look at them in a minute."

Once he got the mattress in place, he took the pages and wandered from the cottage. One glance at Arianna's writing told him that the first several pages were indeed from the diary. Tucked underneath were sheets folded in half. When he unfolded the bottom pages, he realized they were printed-out e-mails, all of them addressed to Arianna.

Logan stopped short, halfway between the main house and cottage as he read the first e-mail. *You belong to me.*

What the hell? Hurrying along the walk, he sat on the porch steps and quickly read through the stack of e-mail.

Stop saying you don't love me... He's not the man for you... I'll have you or no one will...

A chill seeped into Logan's veins. Setting aside the e-mails, he worked his way through the diary entries. The more he read, the sicker he felt inside. *Why won't he leave me alone?... I have to tell Logan...no, I can handle this myself...*

His cell phone beeped, announcing he had a voice mail message. He dialed in to retrieve the message.

"Julie's been in an accident, Logan. I'm on my way to the hospital. I'll call when I know more."

Unease settled in the pit of Logan's stomach. Clipping his phone back on his belt, he grabbed his overnight bag from the Mercedes and headed upstairs. A glance at Shani's desk told him why she hadn't answered her cell—there it sat, connected to the charger. Dumping the bag on the bed, he spied the pad of paper.

Emergency—Julie in hospital, Auburn.

As he swept up the phone to call the hospital, a slip of paper crackled under his foot. He picked it up as he dialed information for the hospital number. Using it to write down the number, his gaze fell on the e-mail address penned on the slip in Arianna's handwriting.

With a shock, he recognized the address—the same one as the author of the e-mails he'd found under the mattress. With half his mind on that further mystery, he dialed the hospital and asked about the status of Julie Mendoza. There was no record of anyone by that name being admitted.

His skin prickling, he called the hospital in the more

northern town of Grass Valley with the same results. Unplugging Shani's cell from the charger, he flipped through her contacts list for Julie's number.

When Julie answered on the first ring, Logan's heart stopped. The story spilled out—Shani's voice message, the note. Julie assured him she'd been home all day. She begged him to let her know Shani was okay as soon as he found her.

Hanging up with Julie, he registered the blinking light that told him there was a message on the answering machine. Instinct told him to press the playback button. He listened, riveted, from Shani's first sleepy hello to her hurried, *I'll be there in twenty minutes.* Then he ran from the room, yelling for the security guard the moment he opened the front door.

By the time Shani passed the golf course, about a mile and a half down Bell Road, she knew she must have missed the shortcut for the hospital. She'd have to pull over, call the hospital to get better directions. Spotting a small country road, she turned left, then stopped so she could dig her cell phone from her purse. But just as she zipped her purse open, she remembered leaving the cell plugged into the charger.

Fine, she'd just go back to town, get directions there. Glancing in the rearview mirror in preparation for turning around, she saw a dark green sedan directly behind her. It had stopped at an awkward angle, nearly filling the width of the narrow gravel road so that it would be impossible for Shani to get around it and back to the main road. She turned to look over her shoulder and realization slammed into her—it was the same Nissan she'd seen following her last fall, the one she'd seen at the crepe restaurant.

Fear shivered down her spine as the driver climbed

from the car. He was slight in stature, maybe early thirties, completely nonthreatening. But as he walked up alongside her car, Shani's heart pounded in her chest.

She crossed her arms over her belly, instinctively wanting to protect the baby. Then just before he reached her car door, she pressed the lock button.

He tapped on the closed window and shouted through the glass. "Are you lost, Mrs. Rafferty?"

The same light tenor as the voice on the phone—she recognized it even through the window. "You're in my way!" she yelled. "You need to move your car."

He pulled something from his pocket; she saw the gleam of metal. Bending away from her, he thrust out. Shani felt the car shift as the air seeped from her front-left tire.

He straightened to face her through the glass again. "Open the window, Mrs. Rafferty."

"Leave me alone!" she screamed.

He stared at her, the pocketknife glittering in his hand. She closed her arms even more tightly around her belly. Up ahead, Shani could see a cattle gate across the road; she wouldn't get far going that way. Barbed wire fencing on either side would prevent her from driving up across the fields flanking the road.

She just had to pray that someone would come by, see the two cars stopped. But a passerby would just as likely think they were two neighbors chatting out here in the country. Would Logan come looking for her? He might go to the hospital, check on Julie.

Except there probably never was an accident. Shani had been the one to mention Julie's name first. This man didn't know her friend at all.

Logan would come for her, she had to believe that. She'd just have to keep this man busy until then.

Swallowing back her terror, her fears for the child she carried, she called out, "What's your name?"

He leaned close to the window. "You know, Mrs. Rafferty. I told you before. It's John."

"When did you tell me? On the phone?" She didn't recall him telling her his name.

"In my e-mails. I told you then."

E-mails…what e-mails? A dim memory surfaced. That single line written on the last page of Arianna's diary. *Three more e-mails today—should I tell him?*

The significance of that enigmatic line hit home. On a hunch, she said, "You don't have to call me Mrs. Rafferty, John. Why not call me by my first name?"

He smiled, blushing. "Thank you, Arianna. I'd like that."

He was the man Arianna had hinted at in the diary. That he and Arianna had never been on a first-name basis implied not an affair between them, but something darker. This man must have been stalking Arianna just as he was stalking Shani.

She watched with relief as he snapped shut the knife and shoved it back in his pocket. He rapped on the window again. "Open the door, Arianna."

She shook her head, and frustration flickered across John's face. He walked away, ambling up the road. Shani wondered if she could get through the cattle gate up ahead if she rammed it with her car. But her flat tire and the heavy chain wrapped around the gate with its sizable padlock made that gambit unlikely.

John crouched, his back to her, then stood again and turned toward her. He supported a rock the size of a soccer ball in his hands. As he came abreast of the side of Shani's car, he hoisted the rock shoulder height. Shani had only enough time to duck, turning her belly away, covering her head to protect it from flying glass as John crashed the chunk of granite through the back window.

As he fumbled for the door lock, Shani put the car in gear, desperate to find an escape. But before she so much as stepped on the gas, John fell backward from the car. Turning, Shani saw Logan throw John to the gravel road. Just beyond him, she saw Patrick Cade and one of his men on the run. Patrick snapped handcuffs on John while Logan hurried over to Shani's car.

It took her two tries to get the door unlocked, she was shaking so hard. Logan all but dragged her out, pulling her into his arms. "Are you okay?" he whispered in her ear.

Now safe in his embrace, she burst into tears. "Thank God you're here."

He lifted her in his arms, carrying her back to the Mercedes. He sat sideways in the passenger seat, holding her on his lap.

"You scared the hell out of me, sweetheart."

She clutched his shoulders, face buried against his chest. "How did you know where to look for me?"

"Your call from that nutcase was still on the answering machine."

She sighed, so grateful to be in Logan's embrace. "Do you know if Julie's okay?"

"I talked to her. She's fine." He stroked her arm. "But you're going straight to the nearest hospital. I'm not taking any chances with our child."

Our child. Joy burst inside Shani at his fervent words.

He drew back, smiled down at her. "But first, I've got to tell you something, sweetheart. I should have told you over the phone, but…I'm an idiot."

He kissed her, then pressed his forehead to hers. "I love you, Shani. With all my heart. I love you."

Epilogue

Spencer Alan Rafferty rushed into the world on June 9, nearly making his debut appearance in the hospital parking lot. A healthy eight pounds, six ounces, Spencer boasted powerful lungs, his biological mother's blond hair and the same lock on his father's heart as his birth mother.

With Logan home for the first two weeks and Mrs. Singh hovering over the baby with complete adoration, Shani barely had to lift a finger. Even now, her feet up comfortably on the living room sofa as she nursed Spencer, Logan kept one eye on her, waiting for his son to finish eating while Mrs. Singh lurked nearby.

She'd scarcely raised him to her shoulder to burp him before both of them closed in. "I can do that," Logan said, reaching out.

Shani smiled up at her husband. "Sit with me. I'll pass him over in a minute."

Logan settled beside her, his arm draped around her

shoulders. Her heart welled with love for him, for the precious boy in her arms.

As frightening as her experience with John had been, even more shocking revelations soon followed when the police spoke to him. A former employee of the alarm company that had originally installed the security at Logan's estate, John had become obsessed with the teenage girl whose family had lived there before Logan bought the place. When the girl moved away and Logan and Arianna moved in, John transferred his obsession to Arianna.

And then to Shani. He'd likely been following her far more often than she'd realized. He'd been the one who'd broken in to the cottage, using his knowledge of where the weak points in the security system were and how to deactivate the cottage alarm.

Even worse, he had been responsible for Arianna's death. The night she'd driven off, angry with Logan, John had followed. She'd apparently spotted him and had tried to speed off to shake him. That decision had had deadly consequences on the sharp curves near Desolation Wilderness.

Shani felt all the more lucky that she and Spencer were alive after such a close call. She passed her now-slumbering son over to Logan. "It's too bad your father wasn't able to meet him." They'd laid Colin Rafferty to rest at the end of April.

Cradling Spencer in the crook of his arm, Logan sighed. "He changed near the end. I got a glimpse of the father he could have been."

"My mother is fit to be tied that she hasn't been able to see Spencer yet," Shani said, laughing. "When she gets here on Sunday, we might not see our son for the entire week she's here. If she didn't love Iowa so much, I think she'd pull up stakes and move into the cottage."

"That reminds me." Logan handed Spencer back to Shani, then rose. He went into his study, then emerged with a manila envelope.

He sat beside Shani again, the envelope in his lap. "I did some research. I know you asked me not to." He stroked a finger across Spencer's cheek. "But after he was born…"

The return address on the envelope caught her eye. An unfamiliar address in Cedar Falls, Iowa. Her heart fluttered in anticipation. "Who's it from?"

"Your son's parents. Your first son. I had a private investigator call them, to see if they'd be willing to resume contact with you. They said yes. If and when you're ready."

Her throat constricted and tears spilled down her face. "Thank you. I'm not ready now, but when I am…thank you."

He kissed her then, his love for her clear in his vibrant blue eyes. She thanked God for the miracle they'd been given, the love between them, the child they'd created.

And the son she would know once again.

* * * * *

Enjoy a sneak preview of
MATCHMAKING WITH A MISSION
by B.J. Daniels,
part of the WHITEHORSE, MONTANA miniseries.
Available from Harlequin Intrigue
in April 2008.

Nate Dempsey has returned to Whitehorse to uncover the truth about his past...

Nate sensed someone watching the house and looked out in surprise to see a woman astride a paint horse just on the other side of the fence. He quickly stepped back from the filthy second-floor window, although he doubted she could have seen him. Only a little of the June sun pierced the dirty glass to glow on the dust-coated floor at his feet as he waited a few heartbeats before he looked out again.

The place was so isolated he hadn't expected to see another soul. Like the front yard, the dirt road was waist-high with weeds. When he'd broken the lock on the back door, he'd had to kick aside a pile of rotten leaves that had blown in from last fall.

As he sneaked a look, he saw that she was still there, staring at the house in a way that unnerved him. He shielded his eyes from the glare of the sun off the dirty window and studied her, taking in her head of long blond hair that feathered out in the breeze from under her Western straw hat.

She wore a tan canvas jacket, jeans and boots. But it was the way she sat astride the brown-and-white horse that nudged the memory.

He felt a chill as he realized he'd seen her before. In that very spot. She'd been just a kid then. A kid on a pretty paint horse. Not this one—the markings were different. Anyway, it couldn't have been the same horse, considering the last time he had seen her was more than twenty years ago. That horse would be dead by now.

His mind argued it probably wasn't even the same girl. But he knew better. It was the way she sat on the horse, so at home in a saddle and secure in her world on the other side of that fence.

To the boy he'd been, she and her horse had represented freedom, a freedom he'd known he would never have—even after he escaped this house.

Nate saw her shift in the saddle, and for a moment he feared she planned to dismount and come toward the house. With Ellis Harper in his grave, there would be little to keep her away.

To his relief, she reined her horse around and rode back the way she'd come.

As he watched her ride away, he thought about the way she'd stared at the house—today and years ago. While the smartest thing she could do was to stay clear of this house, he had a feeling she'd be back.

Finding out her name should prove easy, since he figured she must live close by. As for her interest in Harper House… He would just have to make sure it didn't become a problem.

* * * * *

Be sure to look for
MATCHMAKING WITH A MISSION
and other suspenseful Harlequin Intrigue stories,
available in April
wherever books are sold.

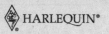

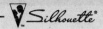
SPECIAL EDITION™

Introducing a brand-new miniseries

Men of Mercy Medical

Gabe Thorne moved to Las Vegas to open a new branch of his booming construction business—and escape from a recent tragedy. But when his teenage sister showed up pregnant on his doorstep, he really had his hands full. Luckily, in turning to Dr. Rebecca Hamilton for the medical care his sister needed, he found a cure for himself....

Starting with

THE MILLIONAIRE AND THE M.D.

by *TERESA SOUTHWICK,*

available in April wherever books are sold.

nocturne™

The Bloodrunners
trilogy continues with book #2.

The hunt meant more to Jeremy Burns than dominance—
it meant facing the woman he left behind. Once
Jillian Murphy had belonged to Jeremy, but now she was
the Spirit Walker to the Silvercrest wolves. It would take
more than the rights of nature for Jeremy to renew his
claim on her—and she would not go easily once he had.

LAST WOLF
HUNTING

by RHYANNON BYRD

Available in April wherever books are sold.

Be sure to watch out for the last book,
Last Wolf Watching, available in May.

SN61785

HARLEQUIN® *Romance*.

presents

The Wedding Planners

Planning perfect weddings...
finding happy endings!

Amidst the rustle of satins and silks, the scent of red roses
and white lilies and the excited chatter of brides-to-be, six
friends from Boston are The Wedding Belles—they make
other people's wedding dreams come true....

But are they always the wedding planner...never the bride?

Who will be the next to say "I do"?

In April: Shirley Jump, *Sweetheart Lost and Found*
In May: Myrna Mackenzie, *The Heir's Convenient Wife*
In June: Melissa McClone, *S.O.S. Marry Me*
In July: Linda Goodnight, *Winning the Single Mom's Heart*
In August: Susan Meier, *Millionaire Dad, Nanny Needed!*
In September: Melissa James, *The Bridegroom's Secret*

And don't miss the exciting wedding-planner tips and
author reminiscences that accompany each book!

www.eHarlequin.com   HRI7507

REQUEST YOUR FREE BOOKS!

2 FREE NOVELS PLUS 2 FREE GIFTS!

SPECIAL EDITION®

Life, Love and Family!

YES! Please send me 2 FREE Silhouette Speäal Edition® novels and my 2 FREE gifts (gifts are worth about $10). After receiving them, if I don't wish to receive any more books, I can return the shipping statement marked "cancel." If I don't cancel, I will receive 6 brand-new novels every month and be billed just $4.24 per book in the U.S. or $4.99 per book in Canada, plus 25¢ shipping and handling per book and applicable taxes, if any*. That's a savings of at least 15% off the cover price! I understand that accepting the 2 free books and gifts places me under no obligation to buy anything. I can always return a shipment and cancel at any time. Even if I never buy another book from Silhouette, the two free books and gifts are mine to keep forever.

235 SDN EEYU   335 SDN EEY6

Name _____ (PLEASE PRINT) _____

Address _____ Apt. # _____

City _____ State/Prov. _____ Zip/Postal Code _____

Signature (if under 18, a parent or guardian must sign)

Mail to the **Silhouette Reader Service:**
IN U.S.A.: P.O. Box 1867, Buffalo, NY 14240-1867
IN CANADA: P.O. Box 609, Fort Erie, Ontario L2A 5X3

Not valid to current subscribers of Silhouette Speäal Edition books.

Want to try two free books from another line?
Call 1-800-873-8635 or visit www.morefreebooks.com.

* Terms and prices subject to change without notice. N.Y. residents add applicable sales tax. Canadian residents will be charged applicable provinäal taxes and GST. This offer is limited to one order per household. All orders subject to approval. Credit·or debit balances in a customer's account(s) may be offset by any other outstanding balance owed by or to the customer. Please allow 4 to 6 weeks for delivery. Offer available while quantities last.

Your Privacy: Silhouette is committed to protecting your privacy. Our Privacy Policy is available online at www.eHarlequin.com or upon request from the Reader Service. From time to time we make our lists of customers available to reputable third parties who may have a product or service of interest to you. If you would prefer we not share your name and address, please check here. ☐

SSE08

SAVE $1.00

Family crises, old flames and returning home… Hannah Matthews and Luke Stevens discover that sometimes the unexpected is just what it takes to start over…and to heal the heart.

SHERRYL WOODS

New York Times BESTSELLING AUTHOR

SHERRYL WOODS

Seaview Inn

"Flesh-and-blood characters, terrific dialogue and substantial stakes…"
—*Publishers Weekly on A Slice of Heaven*

On sale March 2008!

SAVE $1.00 on the purchase price of SEAVIEW INN by Sherryl Woods.

Offer valid from March 1, 2008, to May 31, 2008.
Redeemable at participating retail outlets. Limit one coupon per purchase.

52608272

5 65373 00076 2   (8100)0 11475

COMING NEXT MONTH

SSECNM0308